Get Rich.
Get Even.

Baron Alexander

Wilderwick Press

Forest Row, UK

Baron Alexander/Wilderwick Press
Unit 4 Ashdown Court
Lewes Road, Forest Row, RH18 5EZ
www.baronalexanderbooks.com

*For what shall it profit a man if he shall gain the
whole world and lose his own soul?*
– Mark 8:36 King James Version

*Le secret des grandes fortunes sans cause apparente
est un crime oublié, parce qu' il a été proprement fait.*
– From Le Père Goriot, *Honoré de Balzac*

Behind every great fortune lies a great crime.
– English paraphrase of Balzac's original

CONTENTS

PART ONE
GEORGE ANDERSON

CHAPTER ONE

Empire State Building

"One hundred-second floor, please."

"Yes, sir."

I moved to the back of the elevator as three other couples crowded in. The polished stainless steel folding door was pulled shut and the porter pressed the button. I barely registered the green marble on the walls with its white veins, or the drone of the porter as he repeated the same facts to the excited tourists for the umpteenth time that day. I began to wonder why I even said which floor I was going to. There was only one stop for us from the eighty-sixth floor to the hundred-and-second.

"Smaller than I thought," I said to no one in particular. The elevator had disgorged us. I was surrounded by glass, blue sky, and the cityscape below.

"I know, but it's beautiful." It was a woman with her arm linked in her husband's. She responded to my comment but was talking to him.

I walked next to the thick glass and looked down and all around me. I didn't know what to expect, and found myself recoiling at first.

"Afraid of heights, son?"

I turned around, looking for the source. "Huh?" I soon realized it was the husband of the woman.

"It looked like you just saw a ghost."

"No, I just didn't expect it to drop away like that. There's no opening for me to fall, but it surprised me anyway." I blushed slightly.

"No need to be embarrassed. Is it your first time here?"

"Yes. I'm meeting someone here."

"A girl?"

I shrugged, then nodded.

"My wife and I are here because we saw that movie last year, the one with Cary Grant."

His wife closed her eyes and brought her shoulders up as though she was cold. "It was such a wonderful movie. We saw it twice and I cried both times."

He put his hand on hers and they looked directly at each other, forgetting me for the moment.

"I'll leave you to enjoy the view," I said.

"No hurry, son," he said. "As your gal hasn't arrived, I hope you don't mind us chatting. We're not from New York."

I had gathered that already. New Yorkers didn't start talking to strangers.

"Me either," I said. "And I also saw that movie. It's what inspired me to come here."

The woman's eyes grew wider and began to sparkle. "Ooh, see Tom? I knew it. I bet he's here to ask her to marry him."

I looked down at the floor, my face becoming hot from the word. The little box burned in my pocket.

"I met a girl," I said. "I fell in love. She lives in New York, so I thought this would be an easy place for us to reunite."

"Reunite?" The man was now looking at me. The skyline stood majestically around us through the glass but my story seemed to be interesting them more.

I shrugged again. "I haven't seen her for three months. We agreed to meet here today."

"Just like Cary Grant and Deborah Kerr," the wife said. The skin around her eyes was moist. Her hands were clutching together.

"I hope not," I said. "She got hit by a car and left Cary Grant waiting like a schmo."

The wife grabbed her husband's arm. "This is so romantic. I knew it was a good idea for us to come here."

I didn't want to ask where they came from and hoped they didn't tell.

"Listen, son. We'll let you be. If you need anything, we'll be here for a while."

"Yes, ask us for anything. I want to wait and see what happens." She was already being led away.

I nodded and allowed a smile, my fingers feeling the outline of the box through the fabric of my trousers. I drifted next to the indifferent steel girders that held everything together. I liked being able to see the large bolts and nuts covered with layers of paint. Leaning against the steel, I looked out over the expanse of buildings that fanned out like a floor full of children's toys. My mind drifted along the lines of moving traffic until it rested on the one subject that I hadn't been able to stop thinking about since I met her.

∞

"You plan on going to Harvard?" I was surprised to see a girl on campus.

"Me? No. I'm here because my brother is going. He's a legacy student. My father and grandfather studied here."

"You don't want to?"

"Want to what?"

"Study at Harvard."

Her head turned so that she looked at me out of the corners of her eyes. "Are you trying to make fun of me?"

I felt a cold trickle of sweat form on my lower back. I still couldn't believe I had struck up a conversation with her. I tried not to stare at her riding pants. There were no pockets that I could see, and they were so tight, I thought they were sprayed on.

"Uh, never. Why would you think that?"

"Because Harvard doesn't accept women students. None of the Ivy leagues do."

Her face was slightly flushed. Her blonde hair was long, at least halfway to her waist; it was fashioned back off her face. I became conscious of her eyes and her lips. My shirt was now sticking to my back.

"I didn't know," I stammered. "I'm sorry. I was just trying to…" I didn't want to say 'talk to you'. "Hi, my name is George."

"Barbara. My friends call me Barbie."

Her hand slipped into mine. It was cool. I hoped mine wasn't sweating.

"Nice to meet you, Barbie."

"And you, George."

Her body relaxed again and I could see her hip shifting. I forced myself to look at her eyes.

"Do you know how long this takes?" I was desperate to keep the conversation going.

"Most of the day. My father wants to introduce my brother to all of his old professors. You know, show him around. I'm not sure if this day is for my brother or my father."

"I'm already finished. Do you need to stick around?"

I couldn't believe I uttered the words. I had just met this girl and she was with her family. What was I thinking?

"Not really." She looked to see if anyone was coming down the hallway and out the windows, though I couldn't see what she was looking at or for. It was a massive campus.

"Do you want to join me for a coffee? Or lunch? We can grab a bite at the cafeteria. Will your family be able to find you?"

"I'm not a dog on a leash," she said. Her face had become flush. "I'm sure they'll figure it out eventually."

I nodded, afraid I would say something that would break this spell. I had never done something like this before. She started walking. I followed.

"What are you planning to study?" she asked.

"You're going to think I'm a geek," I said. I could feel my shoulders turning in.

"Hardly. Look at you. You probably played varsity ball; I'm trying to figure out whether it was football or basketball."

She lifted her hand to her face in mock consideration. I smiled.

"Basketball. I never liked the full contact of football."

"Smart. So what are you studying?"

"Economics, but there is something here I want to do more than anything."

"What's that?"

"Computers. You've heard about Mark I?"

"The device that helped the Manhattan Project?"

It was my turn to be speechless. She noticed and raised her chin higher.

"What? You think I'm some dumb blonde girl? I hear things."

"I am impressed. Most girls aren't interested in things like that. I'm fascinated with computers, war, and money. Anyway, Harvard isn't the best place for me to do my undergraduate. I want to be here because of the computers."

"I like a man who knows what he wants."

Her eyes narrowed briefly, and I felt butterflies in my stomach. My body began to shake with adrenaline. I didn't tell her I was here on a scholarship. She held herself like a rich girl. I bet her brother didn't need to worry about how much tuition cost.

We arrived at the cafeteria and I followed her in. She was confident in her movements. I saw the other guys follow her with their eyes as she passed. Either she didn't notice or she expected the attention.

"I'm glad we're not eating in the dining halls."

"Why?" I asked. "They're amazing."

"Not if all you want is a coffee and a sandwich."

"Good point." I would have said the same thing no matter what she answered.

"Maybe you want to try something off campus sometime?"

My insides went liquid. We hadn't spent any time together and she was asking me out. I'd never heard of a girl asking a guy out before. It excited and scared me; I liked it. My mouth went dry.

"Of course," I said.

"I look forward to it."

She smiled at me and my body shuddered with an extra bolt of adrenaline. She was like no one I had ever met. She was smart, confident, and so beautiful I couldn't believe she was next to me.

∞

"I'm sorry, but we have to go. I hope she comes." The man and woman were next to me and it took a while to readjust my senses.

"Thank you. And enjoy the rest of your trip."

I shook the husband's hand and expected to nod to the wife but she also shook my hand. Hers was clammy and cool; I could feel that her skin was papery thin. It reminded me of Barbie's mother's. The smiling couple give me a final wave as the elevator's doors removed them from my thoughts.

∞

"Welcome, George. Barbie's told me so much about you." She shook my hand and looked me in the eye.

"Thank you for inviting me, Mrs. Lexington. Your home is beautiful."

"Oh, you're too kind." She seemed to genuinely flush as she led us through the foyer and into the formal dining room. Everyone was already seated. "You can sit next to Frederick, George. Barbie, you can sit next to your father."

I settled into my seat. I was conscious that it was antique of some sort. If I had to guess, I would say Chippendale, but I had no real idea. I decided not to announce my ignorance and to avoid any direct conversations on money, art, or investments.

"The food smells delicious," I said instead. It was met with appreciative nods.

"Let's say grace," Mr. Lexington said. He bowed his head and rambled off a set-prayer piece I wasn't familiar with.

"Amen," I said in unison with everyone else.

"Tell me about yourself, George. Where are you from, what are you studying, and what are you planning to do in the future?"

"Dad!" Barbie said. "Can't we just eat and enjoy ourselves? George is a friend. He's going to Harvard, and is studying economics and computers. He's going to be someone in the future." When her eyes fell on me, I blushed.

"Oh, well," he said. "I just want to get to know who you are, George. No offence."

"None taken," I said. "I'm just a student right now. I hope to make my mark on the world when I'm done."

Barbie's eyes said all I needed to know. She was proud of me. She was protecting me. It made me want her more than ever.

"You've been seeing a lot of our Barbara," he continued. "I appreciate you coming from Cambridge to us so we could finally meet."

"It's only four hours, and since Barbie is leaving for Switzerland soon, I wanted to spend as much time as possible with her before we're apart."

Mr. Lexington raised his eyebrows but said nothing. Mrs. Lexington's face became soft and I thought I could see her eyes become watery. She looked between Barbie and me. I realized I had another ally at the table. The brother said nothing, probably knowing better than to get in the middle of things.

"How did you two meet again?"

"Daddy, I told you. We met at Harvard when you and Frederick were doing your thing meeting the professors."

"That was weeks ago. Why is it only now that I'm meeting George?"

It was my turn to become uncomfortable. I didn't expect a grilling at the dinner table.

"You've had plenty of chances to meet with him, Daddy. You were always too busy or out of town."

"And you're meeting him today," Mrs. Lexington added. "I, for one, am pleased that George made the effort."

"Thank you, Mrs. Lexington," I said. I was determined to stay in the conversation. "Perhaps we can have a word in private, George, after dinner," Mr. Lexington said.

"Yes, sir. I'd like that," I said.

I focused on eating the roast beef. Everything about the meal, the table, and the room was perfect. I knew they had a staff that took care of these things, and I could see them come and go during the meal, but experiencing it was a very different thing than thinking about it in the abstract. I tried not to worry about what the subject of my conversation with Mr. Lexington would be.

The rest of the meal went as I expected. The conversation changed to Frederick's studies, the weather, the new hula hoop craze that was gripping youngsters, President Eisenhower's making Alaska a new state, and the creation of NASA. I had prepared talking points on all these subjects beforehand. I tried not to be too intrusive, nor too shy. I wanted to become part of the family.

Afterwards, when the dinner and desert were done, I knew the time had come to talk to Mr. Lexington. He caught my eye and indicated to follow him with his head. He didn't need to say anything. Barbie caught the movement and I saw her eyes dart from her father to me to her mother, then back to me. I thought I noticed a suppressed smile, as though she knew what her father was going to talk to me about.

His study was formal, with dark wood-paneled walls. He closed the heavy door against the sounds of the rest of the house and I could understand why he created such a space for himself. It became silent and peaceful. I could smell the cigar and pipe smoke that hung in the bindings of the books and drapes. Along the wall sat a collection of cut glass bottles of whiskey and gin. We sat across from each other on two over-stuffed armchairs. I was glad we didn't have his desk between us.

"So, George."

I waited for him to continue. He didn't. I didn't know what to say. "Yes?"

"Do you want a drink?" He motioned to the whiskey. I knew that was a trap.

"No, sir. I don't drink."

He nodded, lips slightly pursed. "Good. There's plenty of time to pick up vices like that." He got up and poured himself a large whiskey. "Do you want a Coke?"

"Yes, please. That would be nice. Thank you." He opened a door beneath and I could see a small refrigerator stocked with soft drinks and tonics. He removed the cap and handed me the bottle.

"Do you want a glass?"

"No, sir. I like it straight from the bottle. More bubbles."

"I agree," he said, smiling slightly. "But if my wife offers you a bottle, say that you would prefer a glass. She's funny that way."

I put the bottle to my lips, conscious of my faux pas. I remembered a comment I had heard, something to the effect that only babies drink from bottles. I wished I had asked for a glass. It was too late now.

Mr. Lexington sat back and took a sip of his drink. He shook his hand to make the ice cubes tinkle, then took another sip. "My Barbara seems to be very taken with you, George."

I realized then that it was going to be a difficult talk.

"Yes, sir. And I, her."

"Hmm. Yes. And you seem to be a nice fellow, going to a good school. Harvard was my alma mater, as you probably know."

"Yes, sir." My hands were getting sweaty and I didn't like holding the bottle of Coke like a baby. I put it down, careful to place it on a coaster, and wiped my hands on my pants.

"I don't understand your choice of courses, though. Economics, yes, but computers, no. I can't see them being relevant or profitable in the future."

"Sir?"

"I'm merely looking out for Barbara's best interests. I don't know what your intentions are, but I don't want to see my little girl end up with a dreamer without a dime."

I stared at him. I wanted to say as little as possible. I didn't want to correct him or argue. "I plan to study business after I get my undergraduate degree. Everything I've heard suggests that this is the future. The president wants us in space, and we need computers to do that. Slide rules aren't enough. Everything is about large volume mathematical calculations. I want to excel in that, sir."

He didn't say anything for a moment. He took another sip and put his drink down.

"Maybe I'm not making myself clear, George. I don't know much about computers or the future, but I trust Harvard and you're going to be a Harvard man. I'm sure you'll do well in the world."

I didn't say anything. I was prepared to take any compliment he offered.

"I need to know what your intentions are for Barbara." He sat back.

"I love your daughter, sir."

"That's a good start, but it's not enough. My daughter isn't some play thing or distraction for you, or anyone else for that matter."

I began to understand what he was after.

"Sir, I thought we should wait a bit before I asked you, but as you have raised the subject, I think it's only right for me to ask you now." I wasn't prepared for this, but glad that it didn't allow me time to be nervous.

Mr. Lexington sat forward, eyes intently on me.

"Sir, I would like to ask for your blessing to court your daughter and, if she accepts, to marry her." As the words passed my lips, my body became numb. The room closed in on me and everything slowed down. My entire future depended on his reaction.

He continued to look at me, stone faced. His eyes lowered and he turned his head as if he was listening to something. He stood up, buttoned his jacket, and extended his hand. "Good man, George. I would be proud to call you my son. You have my blessing." He smiled.

I tried to stand but needed a second try. My balance was off. I grasped his hand and we shook. We stood, both numb for different reasons, and smiled. I was relieved to feel my hand released. I was only then able to say anything. "Thank you, sir. It means everything to me."

I felt a slap on the back and he chuckled. He seemed genuinely happy, as though he was uncertain of how the conversation would go. "Let's get back to the rest of them before they begin to wonder what we're up to, hey?"

He led the way and I followed closely behind.

Barbie was scheduled to leave in three days' time. It was some form of finishing school where she would learn, definitively, how to host in three languages. She referred to it as bridal school.

"It's to ensure I know how to be the perfect wife," she said, "that I don't embarrass my husband or family."

"I'm sure it's more than that," I said.

She linked her arm in mine. I felt her body against me and it made me uncontrollably happy. We had kissed for the first time a couple of weeks before and she was no longer conscious of how her body rubbed against my arm. Sometimes, I think she did it on purpose.

New York is a magnificent place when you are in love. We strolled the streets and ate hot dogs from street vendors. We window-shopped, went to movies, and spent every available moment together. I couldn't remember a happier time in my life, and couldn't imagine a place I would prefer to be than right there, with her.

"Do you think you'll remember me?" she said.

"I will never stop thinking about you."

"Three months is a long time. A lot can happen."

"Not for me. I've got class and I've got you. I'll be waiting."

"But there will be parties and other girls. You'll forget me in no time." She pouted to make a point.

I stopped walking and held her close. "There are no other girls. You are my soul mate and future. You are the last thing I think about when I go to sleep and the first thing when I wake. I can't stop thinking about you all day. If anything, I'll flunk my courses and get thrown out of Harvard."

She kissed me. "I love you, George. Promise me you won't change."

"I can't change," I said. "You have hard-wired me into loving you."

"Oh, you're such a nerd," she said and kissed me again. I didn't mind.

I enjoyed her soft body next to me. She was slim and athletic but she relaxed into me when we kissed. I couldn't imagine a greater happiness.

"Will you marry me?" The words slipped out before I realized what I had said. She pulled away and looked at me like I was crazy.

"What did you say?"

I knelt next to her and took her hand. "Barbara Lexington, I want to be your husband and your best friend. I want to spend the rest of my life with you. I want you to marry me but don't answer me now. Meet me at the top of the Empire State Building in three months with your answer." I bent my head and kissed her hand. Everything had become blurry and I didn't want her to see me crying.

She pulled on my hand to get me to stand. Tears were running silently down her reddened cheeks. She didn't say anything. She moved closer to me and put her lips on mine. They were warm and wet from tears. I could feel the heat of her body through her sweater. She didn't stop kissing me except to breathe.

When we finally parted, I knew her answer. Her eyes and face glowed with excitement. She was due to leave tomorrow and the thought of it tightened my chest.

"Is that what my father wanted to talk to you about?"

I shrugged. "I'm marrying you, not him."

She held my hand tighter and we began to walk again. She stopped and turned to me.

"Come with me."

"What?"

"Come with me to Switzerland."

"I can't. My classes start tomorrow."

"Come on, just say 'yes'. It's romantic." She was pleading with me like a little girl. Somehow, it made her even more irresistible.

"I can't," I said.

"Just for a week. Or a weekend." She was making puppy-dog eyes at me. My body was exploding with desire for her.

"I can't afford it."

"Sure you can. You can miss a few classes. You're brilliant. You'll make up the work."

"No, I mean I can't afford to fly to Switzerland. I don't have that kind of money."

She stopped playing with me and moved her head like she was emptying water out of her ears.

"What? How? You're going to Harvard. Just ask your parents for some extra money."

"My parents don't have any extra. I'm going to Harvard on a full scholarship."

"Oh."

"But we'll see each other in three months. We can begin the rest of our lives then."

"Yes."

I grabbed her hand and began walking back to her parent's townhouse. I wanted to cherish these last few moments with her before I drove back to Cambridge that night. It would be the last opportunity for me to be with her before we met on top of the Empire State Building.

∞

"Sorry, sir, but we're closing in half an hour. I don't think she's coming."

"Thank you. Let me know when the last elevator goes down. I want to wait."

"Suit yourself, sir."

The city had become dark hours earlier. There was no snow yet and the lights twinkled like a magical story below me. My stomach had been complaining for hours and my joints hurt from standing, sitting, and milling about without purpose. I took one final look through each window and made my way to the elevator.

Just as I approached, the doors opened and I could see the familiar shoe, leg, and dress. My heart stopped and an explosion of hope spread from my chest to my fingertips. I stood straighter and waited for the elevator to empty. As they filed past, the familiar turned into the foreign as the woman's face came into view. It wasn't her. I panted briefly as my body reversed its engines and I tried to recover my composure.

"Down?"

I nodded. There was no up except for a special VIP level on the hundred-and-third, but that was via steep stairs and wasn't for me. I felt my stomach as the mechanical box lowered me to the eighty-sixth floor. I got out and went to the next elevator that took me down the rest of the way. There was a further escalator to navigate past before I reached the street. Worse, there were the smiling porters, guards, and tourists all around me. I wanted to disappear.

The cold air hit my chest as I stepped onto Fifth Avenue. I didn't close my jacket, preferring to feel something other than the numbness of betrayal and loss. I wanted to go to Barbie's parents' house and see if she was back. I looked at my watch. Almost two in the morning. Too late. I decided to walk. I would need to leave for Cambridge in the morning. That left me the rest of the day to get my head around what had happened.

It was noon before I finally emerged from my hotel room. I had booked it in vain optimism that Barbie and I would have stayed there together. Part of me began to think that I jinxed it. I had no right to think like that. Then, I reasoned, if we were going to be married, why not? I shook the hope from my head, dismissing it as fantasy. I thought about what could have caused her to miss our date—especially as it had been three months. We had decided to be romantic, like Cary Grant, and didn't write. It was to be our heart's decision. There would be nothing to stop us meeting up.

But there was.

I took a taxi to their townhouse and climbed the front steps. I heard the doorbell and took a step back. One of the maids answered. I announced who I was and she told me to wait outside. I did.

"Hello, George." Mrs. Lexington looked radiant. It reminded me how beautiful Barbie would continue to be as she aged.

"Hello, Mrs. Lexington. I'm sorry to arrive unannounced, but is Barbie home?"

"Please, come inside." She held the door open and I walked into their spacious foyer. Even the house seemed different arriving without Barbie. It seemed like a museum, populated with fine antiques. "Can I get you some tea?"

"That would be lovely, thank you."

She instructed the maid and we sat down in the lounge. I could see from her face that she was concerned about me.

"How are your studies going?"

"Fine."

"Your parents? Family?"

"Everyone is fine, thank you. And Mr. Lexington? Frederick?"

"They are all well, thank you. I would have thought you'd have run into Freddie at Harvard."

"We run in different circles. He's studying humanities and I'm in economics and computer science. Different parts of the campus."

The tea arrived and was poured. I took mine, as did Barbie's mother, no sugar with a little milk.

"Is Barbie in town?" I couldn't hold off asking any longer. I took a sip and put the teacup back on its saucer.

"She is," she said slowly.

"Do you know when she'll be back?"

"I think you need to talk to her," she said. "When is the last time you spoke?"

I was beginning to feel embarrassed. "Three months ago. Shortly after our dinner here."

She nodded, eyes closed. "We both really enjoyed that day. My husband particularly enjoyed his time with you and the discussion you had with him." She paused long enough for me to understand that she knew exactly what was going on. "You haven't heard anything from Barbie since then?"

"No," I said.

"Not even exchanging letters, updating you on how things were going?"

I felt foolish. "No."

She adjusted herself in her seat and took another sip of tea. "Barbie met someone, George. I hate to be the one to tell you this. You are such a nice young man."

The words began to sink into me like a hail of bullets into a soldier. I knew they were being spoken and I felt them against me, yet they tore through me nonetheless.

"Who? When?" I managed. I didn't dare try to take a sip of tea. My fingers had gone numb.

"A European. English aristocrat. At least that's what she says. He seems nice enough. Oxford schooling, family title, and he asked her to marry him."

"I… I'm pleased that she's happy." I wanted to get out of there as fast as possible. "I don't wish to sound rude, Mrs. Lexington, but I can't stay. I was in New York and needed to come by. I'm very sorry."

She looked at me with an understanding I didn't expect.

"Of course, George. You are always welcome here. I'll tell her that you came." She got up and my visit was over. I thanked her once more and left.

I didn't flag a taxi. I walked back to the hotel where I had parked my car. I wanted to yell, then cry, then smash something. I wanted to know why. I wanted to see her and feel her kiss and body against me. I wanted her to smile at me with her mouth and eyes. I wanted to smell her perfume and watch her walk. I wanted to talk to her and walk hand-in-hand forever.

I wanted, but she didn't. I thought back to our final moments. That perfect time of happiness where my whole world opened before me. What did I say or do that changed all of that in her?

I remembered her warm kisses and tears. I could still feel the fabric of her clothes and the way it lay against her body. I wracked my memory for what could have caused this reaction. I froze as it dawned upon me.

I was poor, or at least not rich enough. I had no substance behind me. I was a risk neither she nor her father would take.

The keys to my future lay in the same word that she found repulsive: scholarship. I was potential; she saw it and believed in me. But she wasn't going to risk her future with a man who could extinguish hers by merely getting hit by a bus while crossing the road. There were plenty of men who were worth more to her dead than alive—provided she was married to them. She wanted—no, needed—a rich man.

I looked at my reflection in the mirror as I entered the hotel. I caught a glimpse of myself in the polished brass of the elevator. As the door clicked shut in my hotel room, I glared at the man in the glass opposite me.

"You will become rich, George. So rich that girls like Barbie will become cheap distractions. Rich enough to do what you want, when you want, and with whom you want."

I saw myself with burning coals for eyes, their sockets blackened and tense. One corner of my mouth lifted, then the other. Soon, teeth were showing.

I would rebirth myself.

Chapter Two

Laos

"Why Vietnam?" her eyes were puffy from crying and her head was pressed into my chest.

"Because someone has to fight those Commies."

"Why you? You graduated *summa cum laude* from Harvard. If you need to serve, the army will give you some cushy position. You don't need to get shot a million miles away in a war no one even cares about."

I looked at Dana. She was a couple of years younger than I was and had her head in the clouds as she studied Milton and Chaucer. I enjoyed spending time with her, especially as she was prepared to move in with me after only three months. She cared for me, but she was no Barbie.

"With my MBA, I'll probably start with a rank of major," I said. "Besides, this conflict will be over soon. I'd never even heard about Vietnam before this."

"Just because Kennedy gets shot, you think you need to sign up? George, this is crazy. One has nothing to do with the other."

"Our president stood up to bullies around the world. He knew that we are judged by our actions, not words."

"And me? Don't you care about me?" She had pushed me onto the sofa and was lying on top of me. She lowered her voice and looked at me through the tops of her eyes. "Won't you miss me?"

"I will." I put my hand gently next to her face and she pressed against it. "But I want to be rich. If I don't do this, I'll be branded a coward. Cowards don't get rich."

"Neither do dead men." She pushed herself against me and sat up. It hurt my legs.

"'Maybe' isn't an option," I said. "We must decide. Say yes and die, or become a hero. Say no and you never live—merely exist."

"You're such a jerk sometimes," she said. She got up and went to the kitchen. I knew that she was getting herself a drink.

"Get me one too, will you?"

"Okay. You're still a jerk though. Beer okay?"

She came back wearing nothing and carrying two beers. The conversation was over.

∞

I enlisted the next day. They told me I would start with the rank of major. It was only when I went to be interviewed that they suggested I join a specialized outfit.

They instructed me to take a lie detector test, confirm my credentials at Harvard, and then told me to sit. I was to talk to a Colonel Starkey.

"Mr. George Anderson?"

"Yes, sir," I said. I stood when he entered. I wasn't sure what I was supposed to do. I looked at the other applicants and saw some suppressed smiles.

"I am not Colonel Starkey, Mr. Anderson. I am here to say that he will see you now. Please, follow me."

I didn't say anything and tried not to feel the burning sensation on my back as the eyes of the three other hopefuls scrutinized my every movement. I wondered if they were even applicants at all. They may have been watching me all along. I didn't want to be paranoid, but this was the CIA.

"Mr. Anderson. Please have a seat."

The room smelled of cigars, although none were lit and the ashtrays were empty. Colonel Starkey sat with his back to the window, which meant that I needed to look directly at the sun when I talked to him. It gave him a corona that surrounded his figure and made it difficult to distinguish his features.

"Is the light in your eyes?"

"Yes, sir, but I can manage."

"If you said no, I'd make you sit where you are. As you were honest, let's sit over there." He motioned to a sofa and armchair. I wasn't sure whether to be thankful or wary. We repositioned.

"Thank you for seeing me, sir. I actually enlisted to join whatever service would have me. I assumed it would be the army."

"You'd be a fine soldier, I'm sure, but we need people who have a head for business, as well as the pedigree that you bring to the table. Harvard has a long history working with the government, military, and business establishments of our great country."

"Yes, sir."

"What do you know about the conflicts we are currently facing?"

"Just what they write in the paper."

"Nothing then."

He waited for my reaction. I didn't give any.

"Do you not believe what they write in the papers, Anderson?"

"Yes, sir. On the whole, they are fine, but I am aware that matters of national security dictate a certain discretion that involves media complicity. Either they know and aren't telling, or they don't know. Either way, the public is unaware of the full story."

"Is that a bad thing?"

"No, sir," I said.

"You don't believe in free press?"

"I do, sir."

"Then how do you reconcile the two?"

This wasn't how I was expecting the interview to go.

"We live in a democracy and we need to inform the public the best we can without creating panic. Information needs to be correct and reported in a responsible manner. If we misinform, we do two things." I raised one finger. "First, we lose their trust." I raised another finger. "Second, we may put our country in danger."

"Who decides?" He was sitting forward, and I could detect a slight uplift at his mouth's edge.

"Judges, congress, and our elected leaders."

"Sounds like a pretty good answer. Do you think it works like that in the real world?"

"I'm here to find out, sir."

"Even better answer, Anderson."

The interview continued for another forty-five minutes and I became less nervous. I was answering honestly and from my gut. *If they like me, I'll join the CIA; if not, I'll join the army*, I thought.

They liked me. I never learned why or what attributes appealed to them most. They knew I was a scholarship student at Harvard from a small town in Illinois. I thought it would be a mark against me, but they saw it as one in my favor.

I was put through the usual training, and shipped off to Laos within twelve months. I was told I would be getting on the job training instead of spending an additional six months stateside. Dana had decided to leave me before I left her but I barely noticed. It was July 1965.

I found myself in Laos, another country I didn't know much about before joining the CIA. I had a vague idea that it was a long strip bordering Vietnam. I also knew that America was not at war with Laos, yet there I was. At first, I thought it was paradise.

"Anderson, I don't want you to get bogged down too much with Air America's operations."

"Sir?" This was another one of those moments when I was given no information and even less time to learn.

The colonel turned to my superior. "I was under the impression Major Anderson had clearance?"

My commanding officer nodded. Colonel Smith continued.

"Air America is a neat little fiction that will allow us to battle the Reds and their pawns. You are aware that President Johnson is ramping up the war in Vietnam. It is up to us to harass and harry the NLF and the People's Army of Vietnam."

"And we're doing that with planes, sir? Are we bombing?" I needed to say something. It was like I was speaking Greek. I felt like an idiot.

Smith looked at my CO again. I couldn't read what the glance meant.

"We'll do whatever it takes, but we aren't bombing. Not Air America, at least. You will find that its slogan, "Anything, Anywhere, Anytime, Professionally," is not just words. Its purpose it to move people, ammunition, and food from anywhere to anywhere."

I didn't say anything. I had read the brochure.

"As I said, you will not bother yourself with that aspect. We have better men equipped to do that."

I raised my eyebrows, waiting for more, and stood still. I had noticed that men were more relaxed here than I had expected at a military base. Perhaps it was because of the civilian nature of the activities. I determined that I wasn't entitled to be relaxed yet.

"You will work with a handful of men, under your command, to come up with the logistics of financing certain delicate missions required of the CIA. We are not officially here, so we don't officially have a budget to do non-civilian activity. I know it's a fiction, but now it's your fiction. Lieutenant Calhoun will bring you up to speed with the operations thus far, and introduce you to Major General Vang Pao."

I stood there, not sure why he had just given me such an important command straight out of training in Langley. He must have detected my hesitation.

"Is there a problem, Major Anderson? Are you waiting for me to ask you to prom?"

"No, sir." I turned and left. My CO remained. I was more wary than pleased. I knew that the way the army or, in my case, the CIA got rid of their own was to promote an officer until they demonstrated incompetence and then dismissed them. Another way was to assign them to a suicide mission. Either way, the undesirable officer was removed. Problem solved. I put these thoughts out of my mind.

Outside was organized chaos. The heat was pleasant, but the humidity made the air into something unlike anything I had experienced before. My shirt already had sweat stains under my arms and stuck to my back. I noticed that not everyone was suffering as much, and determined that it may just be a matter of acclimatizing to the weather.

"I'm looking for Lieutenant Calhoun," I said as I entered the officers' mess.

"That's me," a voice said. He stood and came towards me. He looked like he just came off a Nebraskan farm. He was big, almost as big as I was, with the panther-like walk of an athlete. He slapped a couple of guys on the shoulders as he ambled past, and extended his hand to me.

"I'm George Anderson. I've been told that you'll be showing me the ropes?"

"Yes, Major. We've been expecting you. We don't have the fancy computers that you had in Harvard, but you'll see that we have something even more special."

"What's that?"

"A product universally in demand, a cheap labor force, and no rules—except, possibly, not to get shot." He tapped the inside of his left forearm with his right hand the way the nurse did before drawing blood.

I looked at him in disbelief. My mind was racing through images, trying to understand what his pantomime meant.

"I'm not joking," he said. "Let's talk more about this tomorrow. I'll get one of the pilots to take us up and we'll get you broken in."

"Is this legal?"

"This is the CIA. You're among friends. You don't need to worry that you're being set up. We're all in this up to our necks. If we weren't, our boys in Vietnam would die. It's that simple."

"I don't know the first thing about heroin." I figured out what he was talking about and decided to put it on the table. Half of me was hoping I was mistaken.

"You don't need to. Don't worry about it now. Let's have a drink or three, and head into town to blow off some steam. This your first time in Asia?"

"First time out of the US."

"Then you're going to be blown away. You've never seen anything like it. It took me a few months to get used to it."

"You mean the poverty?"

He laughed and put his arm around me. "The girls."

∞

I was feeling tired from the journey there, but they wouldn't let me sleep. They wanted me to be baptized by fire. I found myself snapping awake a few times on the way to town, usually after we hit an unusually large pot hole.

"Major, do you want dancing or singing?"

"I'll go to your favorite place."

Calhoun smiled and the driver started slapping the steering wheel in time to the radio. I began to regret my words.

There were five of us and there was no door to the establishment, just hanging beads—the type my grandfather put on the garage door to keep the cats and animals out. We were going in, and it was dark. I put my hand on Calhoun's shoulder until my eyes became accustomed. I followed them to a round table and sat down. The lights were red, and I saw movement of what must have been the waitresses.

"Get that one to do it again," said one of the soldiers. I didn't know who he was and I couldn't see his rank from where I was sitting. Then I realized none of us was in uniform.

"Maybe the major's not ready for that on his first day," said Calhoun. I could feel, even if I couldn't see, four pairs of expectant eyes on me.

"Don't mind me. I'll need to get used to whatever is going on here," I said.

That brought some cheers and another soldier put his arm around one of the waitresses and ordered beers all around. I wasn't sure if I saw correctly, but it looked like she didn't have any clothes on.

I began to will my eyes to focus. There were blotches of blackness despite the red light. There were no male waiters, and I was correct; the waitress was naked. I found myself taking in my breath.

"I didn't think we were coming to a brothel," I said.

"Don't worry," said Calhoun. "It's cleaner than the hotels and the marijuana is cheaper than the beer. And," he smiled to his friends, "they are more talented than any waitresses you have ever seen."

He found the waitress he was looking for and looped his arm around her waist. She didn't resist and sat willingly on his lap. He whispered something into her ear and gave her a cigarette and some paper money. I saw her nod and smile. I felt a jolt of warmth—as much from fear as curiosity—when she turned and looked at me.

"You want?" She was staring at me and began moving her body. She was petite, but they all were, and her breasts were smaller than Dana's. I found myself looking at her as I would a train wreck. I didn't want to, but couldn't help myself.

She took my hand and put it on her, then all over her. I felt the fine beads of her sweat against my fingers. She lowered my hand until I realized where she planned to put it. I quickly pulled away. The others laughed as they saw her make me increasingly nervous.

"Relax, Major. Have a cigarette. I think she'll have one too."

She jumped on a chair and I saw her smile. Her midsection was at my eye level. I didn't know what I was supposed to do. I had never imagined a place like this existed. I put a cigarette in my mouth and lit it. She put hers where I didn't think it was possible to smoke. She waited expectantly and I eventually realized she wanted me to light it. My hand shook slightly as I did. I was vaguely conscious of the other four soldiers at the table as they leaned in, trying not to laugh, waiting for the pièce de résistance.

Then it came, and I stared in disbelief. The cigarette end glowed and then the ember was joined by smoke. She continued this for a short while before removing it and putting it to her lips. She smiled, bowed, and accepted more cash for her trick.

"I bet you've never seen that in Harvard, Major."

"Lieutenant Calhoun, you've managed to leave me speechless."

"Welcome to Laos."

∞

The next day was business as usual. I would like to say that I was shocked or saddened by what I had learned during my first few weeks and months, but if Langley taught me anything, it was to understand that the world was all about shades of grey. I met the general, toured the facilities, and flew over the fields. I wasn't there to gather intelligence, obfuscate military objectives, or assist in the war effort. I was there to provide rock-solid American management skills to a logistical dilemma. I didn't expect I would be using my MBA to move drugs around the Laotian jungle.

"I think I understand what is required, Lieutenant," I said after the first full day of touring.

"You aren't doing this alone," he said.

"Do we have cover if things go wrong?"

"You know the drill. Black ops. Deniability. Fifty years from now, they'll still be denying any CIA involvement. If we're lucky, they'll think it was all done by Major General Vang Pao and General Ouane Rattikone."

"How do you keep their names straight? They all sound the same."

"The way they all look the same?" He couldn't suppress a smirk. "They don't. Once you see them as people, you can place the name with them."

"I didn't mean that," I said. "I can't tell whether their first name is their last or if they are old or young."

"You'll figure it out. If you want my advice, sir, you only need to learn the names and faces of the leaders—present and future ones. You can see it in their eyes. Address them, and the rest follow."

"Thank you, Lieutenant. I'll remember that."

"Also remember that the men will follow you if you have what it takes. The colonel wants you in charge. This is your show. I'll do what needs to be done to bring you up to speed. Don't worry, I'm not going to stand in your way when you're ready."

I remembered a lesson that said your enemy always says the opposite to what he means. I put it out of my head. "What is my budget, how many men do I get, and what are my targets?" I stuck to the bare facts.

"You need to create enough revenues to keep a lot of men in arms. These aren't American soldiers, so the costs are less than you would think, but they have to have food, weapons, and ammunition. You need to figure out how to do it and not get caught."

"And make the generals believe they are in control," I added.

"Exactly."

The other lesson I learned was not to share my true objectives. When Barbie left, I set my new goals. There were other girls, Dana being the most important, but they were collateral damage. It only took a week for me to see I was on a springboard that would make my goals a reality. First, I needed to solve the immediate problem for the CIA.

"Timeframe?"

"Yesterday."

"I'll put together my requirements. I'll need two translators."

"Two?"

"In case one gets killed. I don't want to train up a new one. They can be my secretaries as well. They need to be men. I don't want to be distracted and I don't want them to have any ideas. They need to be Americans, not locals."

"And?"

"I'll need to think. You say we have use of Air America?"

"The military will lend it equipment temporarily if it needs anything specific. All of their stock is otherwise civilian quality. We need to appear as though we are keeping to the neutrality truce."

"That shouldn't be a problem. What are our rules of engagement?"

"Like I said, we aren't here. There are no rules." Calhoun paused. "Except one: Don't get caught."

And don't get killed, I thought.

∞

After Kennedy was shot, I thought about enlisting. After my MBA was completed, I did. I went to join the army but was recruited by the CIA instead. I came to Laos to provide administrative assistance but ended up overseeing the growth, processing, and distribution of the only cash crop in Laos—heroin. I had two generals I needed to keep satisfied. They, in turn, needed to feed and arm their troops—not always in that order. I planned to spend a year or two in the conflict zone. I stayed ten years.

It started with sale of heroin to keep Generals Ouane and Vang satisfied. I established an office in Vientiane, the capital of Laos, where I outfitted the IBM 1130 computer system. It gave my operation a sense of legitimacy. No one knew how to use computers and I was able to keep records, monitor shipments, and integrate sales without having an obvious paper trail for people to find. It was the easiest secret-keeping device and was kept in plain view. I hired pretty Laotian girls to sit in the front office as secretaries, and only allowed my team from the CIA into the back office or near the computer.

The generals were efficient and single-minded in their desire to utilize the poppy fields. Opium and its derivatives were the first products, then we built refineries to isolate the morphine and create the brown heroin that would be smoked. My objective was to create number four quality heroin—with the result being a white powdery crystal that dissolved easily and provided the end user the best experience. Value for money. The generals and distributors further down the chain would dilute the purity to increase their profits. The users rarely cared.

The moment I was waiting for happened on 30 July 1967. I knew that a lot of pure opium was arriving from Burma to supply our ally, General Ouane Rattikone. What I didn't expect was the breakdown of the status quo. Until then, Chinese-backed Kuomintang forces took a tax on all opium that crossed the Burmese borders into Laos—usually nine dollars per kilogram. The Burmese were shipping sixteen tons of pure opium and had decided they didn't want to pay the tax. They put everything on mules and transported it directly to the general. As a result of shared intelligence and military aircraft, he was able to fight off the KMT and block their escape. The fighting killed most of the muleteers, who abandoned the opium and their animals. General Ouane got the sixteen tons for free. The KMT were humiliated and forced to leave the border regions, and no further tax would be paid to them. The Burmese warlord lost face and his men abandoned him.

The general needed me to orchestrate sales outside of Laos. I did this as part of my mission. I also knew that my duty would eventually end and this type of contact could help me achieve my goals post-CIA.

What I didn't involve myself in was the general's sale of heroin to American troops in Vietnam. In a way, it helped me in the long term by creating a core group of dependents in the United States for our product. I didn't like it but, on this front, I didn't have a choice.

One of the beautiful benefits of computing is the ability to hide profits through complex transactions. If or when discovered, I would shrug and blame the damn technology glitch. No one cared and soon I was imposing my own tax on all shipments. They were so used to kickbacks to the KMT, local leaders, and national politicians that the modest tax I levied against all transactions wasn't noticed. It was part of doing business, like the cost of calling in helicopters or DC-10s or warships during contact with the enemy. The army had bigger worries and they weren't officially allowed to know anything about actions in Laos. The CIA didn't care so long as it wasn't costing them money. Technically, I should have been court-martialed or shot or both, but I saw my chance and I took it. I served my country and carried out its objectives. In the process, an invisible account in Geneva, via a corporation I set up in Taipei, enjoyed the steady revenues made possible by war, inefficiency, and indifference.

The British government became drug traffickers in the nineteenth century to balance its trade deficit in silver, tea, and opium—the unholy trinity. The United States government was allowing drug trafficking to fund projects for which it otherwise wouldn't have received consent. I was just a toll keeper. Besides, I wasn't a communist. I intended to charge for my services.

For many people, Vietnam was hell. For me, it was an opportunity. There were plenty of enterprising Americans looking to transport the heroin stateside. I was merely the facilitator, standing in the shadows behind the generals. The Americans purchasing our product were bold, paying off people to bring pure heroin in under the bodies of dead soldiers in their government-issued coffins or, more often, inside furniture. Nor did I only sell to Americans. Europeans were just as in need, but the shipping was slightly more complicated. I would sell to anyone and everyone—all to help the Royal Lao Army blunt the force of the People's Army of Vietnam, the National Liberation Front, and their Pathet Lao allies. It was us against them. History will say we lost, but since I didn't exist, there was no way for me to win or lose. I received an honorable discharge for my duties. My file was sealed and wouldn't be available for inspection by anyone. It was just another black-op that would be redacted from the history books for at least a hundred years.

I returned stateside with only one problem: how the hell do I hide nearly a billion dollars of CIA drug money?

Chapter Three

American Woman

"I don't know why anyone bothers," she said. "You can't get rich honestly. And, if getting rich means stealing, then I can do without."

I looked at her tie-dyed shirt and long hair. I thought the hippie movement had long since died, but I wasn't going to say anything. She must have been in her early twenties, wore no bra, and let her hair grow to her waist. The rest of her was covered in near see-through fabric in layers that obscured the body that lay beneath while allowing sufficient glimpses to people like me to confirm that whatever was there was worth the effort.

"Then how does the system keep from falling apart?" I asked. I didn't agree with her, but I had just spent ten years in Laos and I wasn't sure what normal was anymore. Besides, it was heaven talking to an American woman again.

"It's broken already."

"But there are jobs all around us. Your parents probably have jobs. Those people over there have jobs. Our waitress has a job."

"That doesn't mean the system isn't broken. It just means that we've reached a point where the slaves and the masters are able to live with each other in some balance."

I tried not to laugh into my beer. "I've been fighting in Vietnam for your freedom to think like that."

"That's your problem, man. I never asked you to go."

"My girlfriend at the time said the same thing."

"And where is she now?"

I fell silent. Dana left me before I joined the CIA. I wasn't stationed in Vietnam, and I wasn't fighting for her human rights. I was fighting for money. "She left me ten years ago."

"Are you always this uptight?" Her face was an oval, soft, and without the lines of age or hate.

"Listen, Jasmine. You're cool. I get that. I'm not looking for anything and I'm sure you don't want anything from me."

"Chill out, George. You're too young to be this mean. I can see your aura. You're a good man, despite what you think of yourself."

She moved from across the table to sit next to me on our bench. We were outside, overlooking the beach and the benches were low. The sand was cool on my feet and the wind was barely there. I felt her against me as she leaned in and put her hands on my face.

"Why are you so tense?"

"I'm not tense."

"Because of what I said? That behind every great fortune lay a great crime? It's not original. It's Balzac."

"I'm not angry at what you said. In fact, it's something I spend a lot of time thinking about. I've made a lot of sacrifices to make my money. It was important to me when I had none."

"So you're rich?" She traced my face. Her voice sounded mocking, disbelieving.

"I'm not poor."

"Did you make it or take it?"

I thought carefully about this. I had no intention of telling her how I made my money. "Took it."

"Exactly," she said. "They say the best strategy is to choose your parents wisely. Failing that, marry rich. Failing that, steal. Failing that, be content with being poor."

She said it with no guile or anger. She was stroking my face with her right hand and let her left hand drop and feel its way along my body. I felt her lips kiss my neck and I wasn't sure where I was. I hadn't been back long; this type of behavior was something I'd become used to over there, but not here.

"Jasmine?"

"Shh. Try to relax. Try to stop controlling everything for one moment."

I couldn't help but look around to see if people were staring at us. No one seemed to notice. *California*, I thought.

"Do you want to go somewhere?" I asked.

"I want to be here, now. Join me in the present."

I could smell the sandalwood and incense infused in her clothes as she put herself on my lap, facing me. She kissed me and ran her fingers through my military-issue hair. I found myself kissing her back, wondering what planet I had arrived on.

"Who are you?" I asked.

"Shut up and kiss me."

I did. Hippie or not, I wasn't an idiot.

∞

We did go somewhere else. It was a large house set on landscaped grounds behind gates. I parked up next to what looked like the coach house. I followed her up the wooden staircase that clung to the outside of the stone building. I couldn't help but take a peek at the mansion and grounds of the main house. The driveway was at least a quarter mile long and the main road was not visible from the house. It was the type of home I was in the market to buy at some point.

"Do you work here?" I asked as the door closed behind us. The apartment was the size of the triple garage below, but done up in a level of luxury I hadn't expected.

She laughed and pulled me towards her. "Do you want me to tell you that I'm the cleaner?"

I felt myself pulled towards the bedroom. It had a waterbed. I didn't like waterbeds but I held my tongue.

When we were done, her hair covered my nakedness as her head lay on my chest. I found it oddly arousing. I stroked her neck and allowed my hands to trace her body's curves. I loved feeling that space where her waist met her hip. Her body was firm and I guessed she surfed or ran. She didn't look like she worked for a living; her body was too soft and nubile. I waited until later before I asked her how she found herself living in Santa Barbara.

"Mommy and Daddy, darling." She lifted her shoulder and looked over it at me. I liked the way she was so comfortable with her body.

"So, our conversation wasn't just academic?"

"Get over it," she said. "Some people have a talent for making money. Others, for spending it. I'm neither."

"But you like the finer things in life."

"I'd be lying if I said I didn't."

"Could you live with a poor person?"

"Depends on what type of poverty."

"No money," I said.

"Would he be healthy?"

"Okay. I'll let him be healthy."

"Artistic?"

"Who cares? You can read a book or go to a museum yourself."

"You can't be serious," she said. She came back to the bed and put herself under the covers with me. "You can't live without art."

"I can. I do."

Her head went back and looked at me as if for the first time.

"You are an injured bird, aren't you?" She kissed me and the conversation was over.

∞

I must have fallen asleep. When I awoke, I could smell garlic and herbs being cooked in a stew. I hoped she was making meat and not some vegetarian dish. I got up, washed, and joined her in the kitchen. All of a sudden, it made sense why the apartment was so luxurious. Her parents wanted her close, she wanted privacy, and the coach house was the perfect solution.

"Beef?"

"Lamb. I hope you like it."

"Love it." She wore an oriental robe but didn't bother tying it in front. I found it distracting.

"Want to put on some music?"

I looked to where she was pointing and saw the stereo. I found a record out of its sleeve and put it on. I assumed it was something she liked, or it wouldn't have been waiting there.

"I like Led Zeppelin," I said, "but haven't heard this album yet."

"I know. It's pretty serious stuff."

"Physical Graffiti," I read. "I'll pick this up for my-self later."

"You can have mine. My parents keep getting free-bies. I'm sure I have another five somewhere."

I couldn't help but look at her again. She was en-grossed in her cooking, living the life of a princess, and all the while berating the capitalist system that gave her all of these benefits.

"Thanks. Remind me to thank your parents if I ever see them."

"They're too busy chasing money to hang around here." I could see her face tighten.

"That why you hate money so much?"

"I don't hate it, but you can't earn a fortune; you can only take it. If you have a job, you're a loser. If you're a boss, you're just doing the bidding of the owner. If you're the owner, you're probably a loser as well."

"How do you figure?"

"Unless you're big enough, you're probably mort-gaged to your eyeballs. That means you live from one mortgage payment to the next. For some, a couple of months of bad business can wipe them out. Others may take a couple of years. If you're in debt, you're not your own master."

"Is this hippie-speak or did you study economics?" Part of me was agreeing with her.

"MBA from UCLA, thank you very much."

"And?"

"And I prefer to sleep with men I just met instead of whore myself to the banks."

She turned to look at me and closed the distance between us. The lamb was back in the oven, and her robe was barely hanging onto her shoulders. Her green eyes held me until I felt her lips on mine. Her hands were removing my clothes and I was stumbling backwards towards the sofa.

I wasn't sure if this was heaven or hell.

∞

I hadn't meant to meet Jasmine. I was enjoying my time back in the US and thought I'd go as far away as possible from New York. My parents continued to live quietly and contentedly in Illinois and I intended to visit them as soon as I finished in California. It was supposed to be some sun, surf, and good fun. I still listened to the Beach Boys and wanted to learn how to surf. The secluded beach with its sunken restaurant seemed like the perfect staging post to take stock of the locals and decide what I was going to do in the months ahead.

She sat down and started talking. She was free, full of energy, and smiled. I was hooked on her smile until I began to listen to her speak. Only the hippie uniform was incongruous. Then it was her behavior. Then her parents' home. I realized nothing about her was as it seemed.

After three weeks, we moved in together. I bought a four-bed apartment overlooking Central Park. She was happy to join me in New York. I reluctantly admitted that I was becoming happy.

"Look at you!" I stood up when she entered.

"You like?"

"I love," I said.

"Come here and give me some of that love."

She was transformed. I was used to the love child with layers of drug-inspired tie-dyed clothing. Now, she was in a tailored suit with stripes that made her look taller. Instead of a tie, her white shirt was unbuttoned low.

"What happened?"

"I thought you'd like a more appropriately-dressed girlfriend."

"You don't need to change for me."

"I didn't. I was tired of walking into shops and seeing women clutch their bags tightly, or managers rolling their eyes. I guess it was time to grow up."

I kissed her instead of commenting.

"Now, all I need to do is start my own business and my parents will be in love with you." She put her arms around my neck and kissed me lightly, becoming more insistent. She seemed happy.

"I didn't know that you wanted to do anything like that. You know, master, slave, and all that?"

"Don't take everything I say as gospel. I can't believe how much I like it here. The action, the pace, the chaos. This is what I've been missing in Santa Barbara.

It was boring. This place is like sticking your tongue in the light socket."

"Let's talk about what you want to do, and perhaps your parents will want to fund it. Like you said, they'll be ecstatic."

"No," she said abruptly, pulling away. "I don't want their money."

"Then how do you expect to do something?" I was afraid I already knew.

"I was hoping you would help."

She let it hang. We had only just started living together. I thought that was a big enough step. Going into business was crazy. Most businesses failed. She knew that.

"When did I go from being your lover to sugar daddy?" I couldn't believe I said it out loud.

She laughed and came close to me, making sure every part of her was touching every part of me. "I want it all. Don't you know that already?" She kissed me and peeled away to get a drink.

"I'll have the usual."

"Maybe it's time to shake things up a bit," she said.

"Hmm. Okay. You decide. Surprise me."

"I thought I already had."

I walked to the window overlooking the park and studied the scene without definition. My eyes became unfocused and I struggled to see anything but the green, some water, and the buildings that surrounded it. I drifted back to my fear of how to bring my gains into the country. I thought about her shop and began to formulate an idea.

"Okay."

"Sorry?" She was holding my drink and handed it to me.

"I'll fund your shop."

"How do you know it'll be a shop?"

"What else are you going to do in New York? Open up a manufacturing plant?"

"Now that you mention it…"

"Let me know the details and I'll see if I have enough to fund it. We can go over the details later."

"I don't want a gift," she said. "I'm not a whore. It'll be a loan."

"What do you have against whores? Receiving a gift doesn't make you one."

"You know what I mean." She became withdrawn and sat on the sofa. "If this is going to be a business, then I need to treat it as one. Otherwise, I'm no better than all of the others I've been mocking."

I wasn't sure whether this was a point of evolution on Jasmine's part or a more sophisticated tantrum. I liked that I never quite knew what to expect from her.

"You know," I said, "if you don't mind working with criminals, you could use your shop to launder their dirty money."

She looked up. I thought I could see disappointment in her eyes.

"Laundering money?"

"Sell over-priced luxury hand-bags and clothes. They buy it from you, and you give them their money back; they give the goods back—or not—minus your commission."

"What, sell the same goods over and over?"

"Book entries."

"I don't want to replace being a whore to the banks to being a whore to the criminals."

"You really need to tone down on the use of that word. I don't even think it works in this instance."

"How about being a whore to the CIA?"

I went cold when our eyes met.

"What?" I tried to sound surprised.

"You know, the Central Intelligence Agency?"

"I know what the CIA is." My mind was reeling. I needed to slow the conversation down. Or get some air. Or run.

"I didn't want to believe what they were saying about you."

"Jasmine, I don't know what you're talking about." My heart was racing. I was eyeing the door, half-expecting armed officers to come crashing through.

"Laundering money? What the hell are you thinking about? You want your girlfriend to go to jail for some two-bit scheme to benefit some even sleazier gangster?"

"That's not what I meant. I was joking. Please. Forget I said anything." My tightrope was unravelling on one end. First, I thought she knew who I was or what I did. Now, I wasn't sure what to think.

"George, I was beginning to fall in love with you. Why?"

All I heard was the first part. "I love you too."

"I'm not going all gooey on you. At first it was a job. It was nice that you look like you do. You were a gentleman. I didn't think you were going to be able to handle my character."

I took a long drink from the glass that she had handed me. I flipped back to my original fear: She was CIA and I was dead in the water.

"What are you saying? You don't live in Santa Barbara?"

"That's the least of your concerns. No, that place belonged to a client. I've been following you since you returned. They did a personality profile and I came up as the best match."

"So now the CIA is a dating agency?" I was genuinely interested, despite the circumstances. It was clever.

"This isn't a trap, George. See, I'm not wearing a wire."

She took off her jacket, then shirt. She stood up and took off her pants. Only her lingerie and high-heels remained on. I felt a burning inside me. I had never been more aroused in my life. Seated, my eyes were at her mid-section and I could feel the heat coming off her skin.

She saw the look in my eye and stopped talking. She put her left knee on the sofa to my right, and her right knee to my left. When she allowed herself to rest on my legs, my body began to shake. She slowly unbuttoned my shirt and pulled it open. She ran her fingernails across my chest before bringing them up and into my hair. She pulled herself closer, making sure our bodies touched. Her lips traced my face, barely touching. I could feel her heat burning against me. When she finally kissed me, I could feel every inch of my skin. Her touch opened up parts of me I didn't know existed. I forgot what we were talking about as my hands moved up her legs and held her closer.

∞

"For CIA, you sure know your way around," I said.

I didn't see her smile. I wasn't sure if it was even a joke. I watched her gather her clothes and disappear into the bedroom as my eyes became heavy with sleep. I don't know how long I drifted off. When I awoke, I tried to piece together what seemed to be happening. She returned before any answers came.

"We know what you've done," she said. She was wearing sweat pants and one of my t-shirts. She looked sexy as hell.

"I don't know what you're talking about." My heartrate increased. I had survived rule number one—don't get killed—but failed on rule number two—don't get caught. I would replay the recent past in my head when I was safe. For now, I couldn't allow myself to lose my cool.

"I'm not here to convict you. I made a decision today."

I paused. "And?"

"You made it for me."

"Are you going to make me beg for answers?" Her riddles were beginning to aggravate me.

"I am supposed to bring you in so the company can get its money back. They believe they have a better use for it than you."

"What are you waiting for?"

"I think you love me."

"I did," I said.

"I love you."

I was silent.

"I need to bring you in. It's up to you how much you co-operate."

"I haven't done anything wrong."

"Then you have nothing to fear."

"Then why bring me in?"

"There is no way you could have had the money to front my shop or even buy this apartment. I was supposed to bring proof that you had stolen company money."

"That's hardly proof."

"We're not in court. Suspicion can be conclusive."

I was silent. Her softness cut through my protective armor. She betrayed me and would probably do it again. Yet, despite everything, I wanted her to stay. I wanted to believe that she would side with me.

"What did you do? Rob a bank? Steal some transfer payments?"

"They didn't say?"

"No."

"Then you don't have clearance. I'll go with you. It'll give you a promotion."

"I'm thinking of quitting."

I wasn't sure I cared, but my body reacted in ways my mind couldn't fathom; she did something to me. "What'll you do?" My hands were sweaty again. This was my life—probably the end of it—and I was talking to her as though we were discussing the weather over tea.

"Perhaps open a shop in New York."

"Where will you go?"

"I was thinking of living with a hot thirty-something with a mysterious past, a fat wad of illegal money, and checkered history with the CIA."

Her face softened and I looked confused. Her bare feet became visible as she made her way to me, cat-like. She pulled the string on her sweatpants and let them drop to her ankles. She pulled her shirt off in one swift motion and stood before me basking in the sunlight as it poured in through the windows. My mouth tried to make a sound but was met with her lips. As she put her body next to mine, I tried to think who was who's whore. Whoever it was, however it was, the CIA wanted their money back—and they were pulling both of our strings.

Just the Money…

Being a bad boy is good. Being with a bad girl is even better.

Jasmine changed from being a flaky princess brat to a no-nonsense business woman who was determined to make her mark. I liked the hippie version, but I loved her New York sizzle better. Haute couture was all she would wear. I came home to find a tailor waiting for me. She explained that if she was going to look the part, I needed to join in. I did.

"You see them looking?"

"Uh huh," I said.

"Don't turn your head. Assume they're all looking at me, then you."

"Maybe they're looking at me, then you," I said.

She allowed herself a haughty smile and lifted her chin. She was a little too good at this, I thought.

"Can we talk?" She didn't look at me. It was as though she had become a walking mannequin. It was unsettling.

"Now?"

"Later, when we're off the street. Thank you." She tipped the doorman as we walked inside.

"We're off now."

"You know what I mean. A serious conversation."

"Those inevitably end up with us naked."

She turned to me, her eyes mischievous. "*Mais bien sûr*," she said. "But, nonetheless."

I put my arm around her waist as we passed through security and into our meeting. I could barely wait.

After our day's meetings with the landlord of the shop, we finally returned to our apartment. It still had the breath-taking views but no longer felt like I was visiting. It felt like home. Watching Jas step out of her heels, still walking tiptoe, stirred me inside. Seeing her change from her day clothes into her home clothes was strangely comforting. The whole routine reminded me of what I was searching for. It was expensive to live in a New York penthouse overlooking the park, to live with a partner like Jas, and to buy all of the baubles that went along with the role, but it was worth it. I knew it was bought with money, but the feeling that it generated couldn't be bought. This feeling is what I had been looking for my whole life.

"Is everything okay?" She stopped mid-step as she noticed me staring at her.

"Of course. I was just admiring you."

"It looked a little creepy."

"You know how to take the man out of romance," I said.

"You love it."

"I do."

"You love me."

"I do."

"But you won't."

"What?" I enjoyed the way she lulled me into a comfortable mental space before she came next to me. I loved the way she smelled and felt. Then, I felt the sensation of sand churning in my stomach. I knew that feeling; I wasn't entirely surprised. I just thought we'd have more time together.

"Remember what we were talking about a while back?"

"Buying that building?" I played dumb.

"No, before."

"When?" I wanted her to say it.

"When we just arrived."

I inhaled sharply. "That's ancient history."

"That was a hiccup in my mission."

I felt a tentacle of cold creep along the inside of my left arm. "Mission? I thought you quit." I said the words but didn't believe them. The CIA had taught me to lie and betray. I wanted to unlearn those skills. I watched Jas play me and I tried to convince myself that

I was over-reacting. I willed myself to love her and remain blind.

"George, I love you; I always will. These last few months have been the best times of my life."

"Oh, shit. Here it comes."

"No, not that. I'd marry you if you'd ask me, but you're going to hate me soon enough."

My body didn't know if it was going up, down, or sideways. "Marriage?"

"In a different life. I can't be the Bonnie to your Clyde. Sorry, George."

"What the hell are you talking about?"

"I don't know how you can afford the millions we spend—on this apartment, the investments, everything."

"I thought you were on board?"

"I thought I was too."

"What are you saying?"

"I need to call it in."

I looked at her. Her face lacked any humor. She was company through-and-through. She was kidding herself as much as I was. There was only one way this would end.

"Can you give me a head start?"

She looked at me and I saw the first tear fall. She shook her head.

"I can't."

I was calm. Everything I had scammed, lied, and stolen was about to be taken. Yet, I felt nothing. I didn't even feel betrayed. In some ways, I was thankful.

"Can I keep anything?"

She shook her head. Tears were flowing silently.

"Can we…?" My voice trailed off. I realized my emotions for her weren't fake. I felt the stab of betrayal as it went from theoretical to real in my mind. I didn't think I could still feel like this.

I saw her lower her head. Her hair fell forward and all I saw was her curved back. It shook a little.

I got up and walked to the window. I thought it was a good thing they didn't open; I wasn't sure if I could trust myself. I looked into the distance and began tracing the buildings around the park with my mind. The park became a green patch in my blurred vision. It morphed into the jungle of my past. I saw men marching off into the jungle, paid for with the heroin that I sold—that the CIA sold.

"I did nothing wrong. I want you to know that."

I didn't hear a reply. I was still looking out the window.

"I did what I was told to do," I said. Still nothing.

Air America, the two gook generals, all those dead men. Life was like a blurry dream for me then, and it was becoming so again. I thought I was smart enough. I don't know how anyone could have found me out.

I turned around to see her. She hadn't moved. I walked past her into the bedroom. I grabbed my gym bag and filled it with the cash I had in the apartment. I added two handguns and four clips of ammo. The other suitcase was already packed. I made it a habit to keep a freak-out bag in the event I needed to move quickly. Today was such a day. I changed into a pair of jeans, flannel shirt, and brown bomber jacket. When I walked back into the lounge, Jasmine stood.

"Where're you going?" she asked.

I put a business card in her hand.

"What's this?"

"My lawyers," I said.

"What am I going to do with this?"

"Call them when you have a deal with the company and a presidential pardon."

"I could take you now."

"You could, but you'll never get the money. They don't want me. They want the money."

"How much is there?"

"Enough to make it worthwhile to get a presidential pardon."

I walked to the front door.

"George, wait."

I turned and tossed the apartment keys to her. "Stay here until it's done. I'm not coming back."

"Where are you going?" She was next to me. I barely noticed her moving as my eyes battled the red mist.

"I don't know."

"Will I see you again?"

I laughed. "Jas, you're good, but not that good."

She leaned forward, body limp, trying to put herself in my arms or kiss me. I couldn't read her anymore. I didn't care. I turned, opened the door, and left. The last thing I heard was the click of the door closing behind me. I was relieved it wasn't a bullet passing through my brain instead. *The money*, I thought. *All they want is the money.*

Chapter Five

To be a Banker...

Part of me was relieved to be rid of the burden of such a lot of dirty money. The other part mourned the loss of the empire I could have built. I consoled myself that I was still young, only thirty-six, and I was alive. I had also kept an extra secret stash of money for just this situation. It wasn't much compared to what I lost, but it would keep me alive and able to pursue the life I've always wanted. I called it the gangster's getaway money. I never thought I'd need it.

Jasmine called my lawyers within the week. A week later, I was a free man, pardoned and unblemished. And alive. I half-anticipated that I'd end up in the foundation of a new skyscraper or dissolved in a bathtub. I decided to return to the only place I still felt safe. I went home.

"Georgie!" I could see her hands were wet, probably from washing dishes. Her eyes lit up when the door opened.

"Hi, Mom."

"Frank! Frank! Come in, son. Frank!" I was surprised at how loud she was able to yell when she wanted to. "Your father is going deaf and I'm going hoarse. Put your things over there. Don't worry. Oh, I can't believe you're actually here."

She hugged me again and disappeared around the corner to find Dad.

"My boy! Come here and give me a proper bearhug." Dad had put on a few pounds and he hadn't shaved for a couple of days, but he looked good. I was surprised at how strong he was able to hug me.

"Hi, Dad. Surprised?"

"You can surprise us like this anytime. Do you want a coffee or tea? Perhaps some ice cream? We just got two tubs from the store. One's butterscotch ripple and the other is cherry. How about a scoop of each?"

I looked at the two of them as they became fully animated. They began cleaning and clearing things that made no difference to me whether it was on the table or counter or bookshelf. I sat at the kitchen table with a mug of steaming black coffee and an obscenely large bowl of ice cream. They had the same.

"I needed a break from the craziness," I said after a few spoons of ice cream. I wasn't fond of either flavor at first but by the third spoon, I was beginning to like them.

"You stay here as long as you like. Your room is always waiting for you."

"Thanks, Mom."

"Do you know how long you'll be here?"

"Couple of weeks, if that's okay."

"How can you talk like that?" She feigned anger. "Everything we have is yours. Everything we do is for you."

I nodded sheepishly and had more ice cream. I put another spoonful of it into my coffee.

Dad was silently eating his desert and watching me talk to Mom. When he finished, he sat back with his arms up and fingers linked behind his head. It was part stretching, part ritual. I did the same thing.

"Is everything okay, son?"

"Could be better. Jasmine didn't work out."

"I'm sorry to hear that. She seemed nice. A bit flaky, but in a good way."

"I know what you mean. She grew on me."

"How are you coping?"

"Tougher than I thought. I also had some skeletons from back in my service pop up."

"You don't need to say anything, George. We don't need to know details."

"I wasn't going to say. Safer for you and me." I smiled. They had no idea.

"What kind of skeletons?" Mom asked.

"The kind that wiped out almost all my savings."

"Do you need anything? We can always refinance the house." Dad sat up and leaned forward.

I forgot how quickly they were willing to give everything to me. The scholarship was the only way I could have gone to a school like Harvard. Even then, they were prepared to sell the house if it meant a better education for me. I wondered what they thought of my enlisting. I never asked; I doubt I ever would.

"Thanks, Dad, but it's not that bad. I'm aggravated that I lost most of my nest egg. I was trading while I was over there. I made some money. The government says that it belongs to them because I earned it while on their time." It wasn't the whole truth, but close enough.

"I've heard about this kind of thing happening at universities," Dad said. "A professor invents something and the university gets the benefit because it was done on their time."

"Maybe Jas was right," I said.

"About what?" Mom asked.

"Perhaps we're all slaves. Of sorts, anyway."

"Son, we're all slaves to the clock."

I let that one hang. I wasn't sure whether Dad was trying to be philosophical about mortality or commenting on the working life.

"I'll tell you one thing, George," he continued. "If I were to do it over and I knew what I know now, I would do everything possible to get into banking. Better yet, own a bank."

He used his spoon to steal some ice cream from my bowl. I got more than him and I ate slower. Mom noticed and stood up to get a refill for him. I watched their peaceful movements. No language was needed, just the practiced observations of each other's behavior.

"I bet it would cost a bundle to open a bank," I said. "But what an idea."

"Not as expensive as you'd think. You can get one of those banks in the Caribbean for fifty thousand dollars as long as you could show some substantial assets, say, a million bucks of property."

"It may as well be a billion, Dad. I might be able to swing the fifty grand. The rest is not possible anymore."

"What if I let you list our farm as your asset? I'm not sure how the whole thing works, but if I was going to trust anyone, it would be my Harvard-educated son." He glanced briefly at Mom and I could feel her nodding back.

"That sounds great, but let me hang out for a bit before we start our banking empire."

"Wouldn't that be something," he said, almost to himself. I didn't realize that this was his unrealized dream.

"I'll look into it tomorrow. We can see if it makes sense. Besides, I'm looking for a project."

"Great. Enough of that. Want to catch a movie and relax?"

∞

A month later, we strolled into Plymouth, Montserrat, with a cashier's check for ten thousand dollars. After minimal research, I realized that a banking license only cost ten grand. My dad seemed a little disappointed that he wasn't going to put the family farm on the line for me. I gave him ten percent of the bank to make him feel like he was part of the adventure. Besides, I thought at the time, it was his idea.

I met with a solicitor who agreed to act for the company in all legal matters. He also agreed to hang my shingle outside his office. I had two bronze plaques made, each the size of a ruler. One was placed by the outside door so that all the world could see it. The other was placed on a filing cabinet into which all my documents would reside. For all intents and purposes, that filing cabinet was my bank.

We shook hands and I was directed to an accountant. Naturally, it was a friend of my solicitor. I ensured that he was suitably instructed and we opened an account at Bank of America. As my new bank was barely a filing cabinet and had no actual employees, it was impossible for me to accept or deposit cash or wire money. This is where my new correspondent bank came in. Bank of America would fill that role until we were able to do it ourselves. The International George Anderson Bank was born. As I didn't want my name spelled out, I shortened it to The IGA Bank of Montserrat. I hoped having a tiny bank, in a tiny jurisdiction wouldn't make them come after me. If they did, I was pleased I had a presidential pardon. It may not have been a get-out-of-jail-free card, but it allowed me to start a new life with some degree of confidence.

"Doesn't seem very exciting now that it's done," Dad said. Mom decided to come along for the adventure and was quietly enjoying watching us work together.

"It's no different to any company, Dad. We needed legal status. We have it. Now, we need to find customers."

"I'll be your first."

"Our first. You're a ten percent shareholder."

"Okay. Details. When we get home, I'll see what I can deposit. I'll ask my friends. Oh, what interest are we going to give them?"

"We can attract deposits with higher interest than other banks. We don't have their overheads."

"As long as we earn more by lending it out."

"And they don't demand their cash back. Otherwise, we'll end up with a run on our new little bank."

"I'm sure you'll figure it out. I'm looking forward to coming here for vacations. Company expense, naturally."

"Of course." I was enjoying the gamble, but realized that if we didn't find deposits, we would be dead in the water.

∞

The elation of being the owner of a bank wore off after six months with no deposits. I felt like those authors who write books no one reads, or songs no one sings. I had a structure but no fans.

I was back in New York in an anonymous bar called The Club. My meeting was a no-show and I was enjoying a drink by myself. The bar was dark and set back from the marbled floor that gleamed in the bright lights near the elevators. I was far enough inside so there was no way to see me from the hotel that connected to the bar. Or was the bar connected to the hotel? I was tired of over-analyzing everything.

"You need that chair?"

The voice startled me. I looked up to see a medium-built guy with a black slash for a moustache. I kept myself clean-shaven partly because I couldn't grow a reasonable beard.

"No. Knock yourself out," I said. I became aware of him and his friends. I had been sitting there for over half an hour and had a few drinks into me. My mind was focused on how to get people to part with their money. I couldn't understand why someone would put their assets in my bank instead of their local state or federal bank. What service did I bring to the customer? Anonymity? Better interest rates? A great filing cabinet? I was beginning to think that I should walk away from the bank idea when I saw Richard Pryor join their table. I vaguely knew who he was from a record of his stand-up comedy I had received as a gift. What was it called? Something crazy nigger? I laughed despite myself when I listened to it. I decided to talk to him.

"Sorry to disturb you, but are you Richard Pryor?" I don't know why I did it. Perhaps it was the club. Perhaps it was me being alone next to a party.

"Who the fuck are you?" He wasn't angry. The words just spilled out of him.

"I'm a fan. I got your record for a present and couldn't stop laughing."

"You think it's funny to laugh at niggers, honkey?"

I looked at him, then let my eyes drift to the group of onlookers. Their eyes were moving from me to Richard, their faces expectant. I wasn't sure of what.

"I just wanted to shake your hand. I haven't had an honest laugh like that since Laos."

He looked at me, about to unleash a fury of expletives, then stopped himself. "My man. Always happy to meet a fan. Jon, do you know this cracker?"

"Never seen him," a voice said. "Oh, yeah, I just took a chair from his table."

"Then he's like all the rest of us. Some oppressor is always taking chairs from our fucking tables." He turned to me. "What's your name?"

"George."

I saw him about to say something, then changed his mind. "George, nice to meet you. You already know me. That's Jon over there. He's a vet too. And the rest, I don't know."

I nodded at everyone and took my hand back after shaking Richard's. Now that I was next to them, I could see that the women were too beautiful for the men they accompanied. Either the men were exceptionally rich or the women were on the meter. I made to leave.

"Have a drink with us," Jon said.

I turned to see him motioning me towards his table. It was covered with glasses, ashtrays, and partially smoked cigarettes. He had a woman on each side, his arms around them. He sat back in the booth like a king surveying his domain. I couldn't understand why he would have been the one to ask me for a chair when he could have had one of his flunkies do it for him. On my former chair was a mountain of a man. I assumed it was his bodyguard. He didn't say anything. There were three other men, each with two women. They had moved a round table next to the booth and clustered together. The two unattached women went to Richard.

"I don't want to interrupt your party," I said. I regretted it, but I was trying to understand what type of people I had bumped into.

"Not at all. I insist. You know, let's get out of here. There's no bloody room, and we're huddled around these tables like some teens in high school." He began to move and everyone was set into motion. He wiggled out from his booth and I saw him throw some bills on the table as he left. I had nothing better to do, so I followed.

"So you were in Laos?" He was casual, but he looked me straight in the eye. I could see that he was fearless and curious at the same time. He was the alpha male but he didn't act like he knew everything.

"Yep, from '65 to '75."

He stopped and put his hand on my arm. "You serious?"

I shrugged. "Yeah. It was intense."

"I don't know anyone who was there that long. Who were you with?"

"Special Ops."

"That doesn't mean anything to me," he said.

"I can't give more details. It was classified."

He looked at me a moment longer than I was comfortable with. "What are you doing now?"

I hesitated. I shouldn't have been there. I was beginning to get the feeling that these guys were gangsters or criminals of some sort. I didn't need this type of trouble. "Banking."

"Manager? Which one?" He was walking again and we were in the corridor between the club and the elevators to the hotel rooms.

"Owner."

He stopped again. "Which one?"

"It's relatively new," I said. I didn't want him to think the ink was still wet on the company's articles. "Called IGA Bank of Montserrat. Based in the Caribbean."

He stuck out his lower lip and concentrated on something. The others were already entering the elevators. "You interested in growing your bank?"

"Of course."

"Are you in New York visiting?"

"I live here."

"Good." He rubbed his moustache. "Good."

I stood there like a lemon. The elevator had already taken the others somewhere and I was alone with Jon while his bodyguard hovered three paces away.

"Are you able to take cash deposits?"

"Yes, of course. I use a correspondent bank."

"And they'll work with you, no questions asked?"

"Yes." I didn't really know the answer to that, but I wasn't going to sound equivocal.

"What are your charges?"

"It depends on what services you require." I was starting to get excited. The hardest client was the first.

"We can't talk here. Let's go to the party and meet up tomorrow to discuss. I'd like to work with a fellow vet."

∞

The next day started at four in the afternoon. The party was held in adjoining penthouse suites, and guests kept arriving until it was standing room only. People smoked marijuana like cigarettes. There was cocaine and endless champagne. I don't remember any food, but there must have been something. As the night progressed, both men and women began to feel obliged to disrobe and run around. Some were chased into a room; others told to put their clothes back on. I tried to be next to Richard, but he wanted his girls. Same with Jon. I ended up jostling with what looked like investment bankers and gangsters. I couldn't tell which were which.

I woke up entangled on the couch with a girl who couldn't be more than eighteen. I felt a sadness and a loss of innocence I didn't expect. She could have been Barbie, or Jasmine, or me in different circumstances. She had parents, maybe a boyfriend. Instead of enjoying a movie and popcorn, she was here for rent—on her own accord or not. Her body would be lustily enjoyed and shared. As she aged, she would be discarded like moldy bread.

The sun hurt my eyes and I wondered how they could live without blackout curtains. I didn't think it would be cool to wait around until Jon woke up, so I scrawled my details on a paper and stuck it on the television screen. Someone would see it. He'd call or he wouldn't. If I had learned anything in life, someone like this didn't respect a person who crawled to him on his knees.

My apartment wasn't far from the hotel. Ten minutes by cab. I showered, changed, and dropped to road level to visit my local greasy spoon. I was starving. As I was about to eat my first mouthful of eggs, Jon Roberts walked through the door.

"George," he said. "Sit, please. Mind if I join you?"

"Please. Mind if I eat?"

He waved his hand and I continued. The waitress came over and poured us coffees. The bodyguard sat two tables away, facing the door. He ordered a full breakfast with his coffee.

"Surprised to see me?" he asked.

I was, but now that he was in front of me, I felt comfortable. I knew I was working with a professional—or someone very paranoid. I nodded. He liked that.

"I hope you don't mind. I had you followed. I've also made some calls about you. I've learned a few things. I have to say I'm a little surprised."

I swallowed hard. The toast became dry and stuck in my throat. I took a sip of coffee.

"CIA? Is that why you couldn't tell me?"

I shrugged. Even if he guessed, I wasn't allowed to talk about it.

"Don't worry. I know you don't work with them any longer."

He looked at me, waiting for me to say something. I didn't.

"I'd like to discuss some business with you."

"Go ahead," I said. "It may not be the most professional office, but there's no one here."

He looked around to confirm, then leaned in. "I have a very specific need and partners who are not the forgiving type."

I nodded, finished my plate, and pushed it aside. I downed my coffee and put it to the edge of the table for the waitress to refill.

"From what I can tell, you have the education, experience, and temperament to do this, but I still don't know you from Adam."

"I can't change that," I said.

"I know, but I also believe that fate has brought us together."

"I don't know if I believe in fate," I said.

"It doesn't matter. We're sitting here now."

I was silent. He didn't look stoned or drunk.

"I have a cash flow problem," he said. "And I think you can help me."

"I don't have liquidity or cash reserves to lend you money at this stage," I said. I felt disappointment creep into my legs as I began to fear that my first client was slipping away. I wanted deposits, not mortgage requests.

"Not like that. I have cash that I need to deposit into a bank with discretion."

He let the sentence hang. I tried desperately to look cool. To give me time to think, I looked for the waitress and indicated to my cup that I needed a refill. We sat in silence as she came over, cleared our plates, and topped up our cups.

"I can do that," I said finally. "How much and how often?"

It was his turn to be silent. "It will vary. Numbers are big. You will need to determine a way to spread this out. You can't do it all through one corresponding bank."

"Okay. I'll figure it out. That's my job."

"Listen, George," he said, suddenly animated. "This isn't a job. If you take this on, you need to be one hundred percent committed. These guys don't fire you. You get dead in a way you don't want to."

I had figured that out on my own. "Can't be worse than what I did back in 'Nam." I realized that I said Laos earlier and it was probably what he picked up on. That's why he thought I was CIA. We were never officially in Laos. I had to give him credit; he wasn't an idiot.

He pulled out a cigarette and lit up. I waved away an offer for one. "You don't have to pretend in front of me, George. I know what you did. Do you think I'd be talking to you like this if I didn't?"

I had no intention of falling into a trap.

"Let's leave that conversation for another time, hey?"

He wouldn't. He was like a dog with a bone. "You know, Vietnam terrified me so completely, I can no longer feel fear." He took a long drag from his cigarette to let the sentence sink in. "I did two tours. That's a long time. I didn't want to come back. I didn't think I would fit in."

I found myself nodding along, despite myself.

"But I did. And the world was different. Not the way most people might think. I could see things clearly. I had an opportunity, and I moved on it. Now, I'm reaping the dividends. You can get rich, but you can get dead just as easily."

"What do you want me to do, Jon?"

"I'm getting to that. I can't believe that you stayed for ten years in that shithole. Lucky for me, I have a little information on you. I couldn't get full details but I'm going to guess."

I waited.

"You were logistics."

My mouth went dry. This was impossible. There was no way he could have access to this information. It must be a guess.

"And your product helped fund our enemy's enemy."

I took a sip of my coffee. This wasn't happening. Who the hell was this guy?

"I figure I need to find a banker who is not solely interested in the cash, but someone who understands the delicacy of the operations being conducted."

"Jon, we don't need to dance around the subject. I can't talk to you about things that went on over there. I can't confirm or deny anything. If you have checked me out, great. If I can be of some assistance, even better. I don't scare easily and I am comfortable with complex structures. I don't have a big staff, and I am paranoid about security, confidentiality, and loyalty."

I stopped talking and hoped I didn't speak out of turn. I realized Jon was connected to something—mafia? I didn't think he was CIA. But, then again, I wasn't not sure what anyone did anymore.

He began to grin, his teeth filling his face. His moustache became a thick line above the lip. I thought he must need to shave twice a day. The thing that caught my attention the most was his eyes. They weren't grinning.

"George, it's not my money, but they are my contacts. I'll start you with a million a month cash. If you can handle that, we can increase it over time."

"That's a lot of money. Yes, I'll do it. Of course, I'll do it. Let me work out the details and…"

"Don't sweat it, George. I'll give you a few days. I'll be in touch. You're a smart guy. Any bastard who stayed in Laos for ten years is one mean sonofabitch. You'll be a good addition to the team."

"Hang on," I looked him in the eye. "I can't be part of your team."

"What?" He stopped mid-way as he was about to leave.

"I mean, I want to do business with you, but as a bank. I'm no good to you if we don't have an arms-length relationship."

"That relationship turns into a hug after the first couple of deals. Those arguments don't work."

"They do if we're careful. Think about it. Your clients aren't idiots. They have their own objectives.

Neither you nor I need to worry about that. We are interested in logistics; how to get a product from A to B, then to ensure that payment is received in a way that can be used. Cash is great but useless if it can't be spent. I need to know what kind of discount your clients and you are going to be satisfied with. And where do you want to access your money? In the US? Switzerland? Bahamas? Do you want everything converted to diamonds, gold, or a combination?"

"Whoa, bro. Relax. Let's talk about that later on. Today was just a meet and greet. I think we know where each other stands. We'll make this work."

He shook my hand and left. I watched him leave, not knowing if this was the most exciting thing I had ever done, or the stupidest.

∞

Jon Roberts wasn't his real name. I couldn't find his birth certificate. I was told he was born to a Sicilian called Nat Riccobono, but he changed his name after his father was deported back to Sicily. His family was heavily involved in the mafia, but Jon seemed to be his own man. From everything I could tell, he was a violent young man who got into trouble and was heading to jail but did a deal with the US army. They erased his records in return for him going to Vietnam.

"At least he wasn't lying about that," I muttered. "Perhaps his mafia connections go as high as the CIA. Naw, just a lucky guess." I had a habit of talking to myself. I hoped I didn't do it when other people were around.

I still had my own sources—military police, CIA, and the generals. They didn't know about my private tax or fall from grace with the CIA. They treated me as the officer I was. I got my information and I owed them one. I knew they would collect at some point. I just hoped I would be able to deliver when they did.

We had our meeting on the appointed date. We squared away the finer points of how the cash would need to be packaged, labelled, and accounted for. I decided to deposit a maximum of one hundred thousand dollars per account per branch per month into IGA Bank of Montserrat via Bank of America. Once it had been converted into a book entry, I would have the funds transferred to the New York branch, which would transfer one large sum, preferably over a million dollars per transaction, to Bank of America in Montserrat. My objective, I told Jon, was to become large enough not to require a correspondent bank. "Let's do the first transaction before you build your empire," he replied.

He was smart, and he had a problem. He had a lot of cash to move. I remembered the panic and excitement that hit me in Laos when I realized the scope of the business we were doing. It didn't take me long to understand who Jon's clients were: Colombians. More specifically, the Medellin cartel. I experienced the same tingle I felt years before when I realized that this was the ticket to becoming enormously rich. It was up to me whether I learned from my mistakes or if I was stupid enough to make the same ones again.

Chapter Six

Griselda

"I don't need to meet her," I said.

"You don't have a choice," Jon said.

"It's not good for business for me to get too close."

"She doesn't ask twice. You won't be in business if you don't go."

I had heard enough about Griselda Blanco to know I had no choice.

"If you don't go, she'll think either you're cheating her, or you don't trust her, or both. We've been doing business for almost six months. She's moving serious coin through your bank. You wouldn't exist without her."

I had to agree. The first transfer was nerve-wracking. I agonized every detail. I spread deposits far and wide. I needn't have worried; no one cared. They were dealing with a bank, and who my customers were wasn't their concern. Jon had floated the idea of increasing cash deposits to twenty million per month and was concerned that I couldn't handle that amount. Naturally, I said I could. Griselda demanded a meeting.

"Jon, I have to be honest with you. She scares me. I know it's not cool to admit this, but her reputation is a bit heavy."

"Heavier than the gooks in 'Nam?"

"At least we knew we could kill the bastards if they got out of line. More likely than not, she'll kill me just to amuse herself."

I watched him to see how he took my admission of weakness. He shrugged. "You're selling yourself too short, bro. Just be straight with her. She'll only kill you if she thinks you're lying or cheating her."

"In for a penny, in for a pound," I said. I had heard the expression and liked it.

"That's the spirit."

"When does she want to meet?"

"Tonight."

I tried to stay calm. Just another client. Psychotic, irrational, and rich. In some ways, she was worse than the CIA. She had no rules and fewer objectives.

Jon picked me up later that evening. He liked to drive. He drove two speeds: Seventy-five miles per hour on side roads and a hundred and ten on the highways. It felt like we were in a car chase. He wasn't reckless, just fast. We arrived at a low-slung ranch house in the suburbs of Miami. There were no gates or security. Anonymity and moving constantly was her security.

"You have any heat on you?" Jon asked before he turned off the engine.

"No, do you?"

"Of course, but it's better if you don't."

"This isn't making me less nervous."

"Don't worry. You'll love her."

I followed him into the house, was patted down by guards, and shown into a room that had a sunken portion that I had to access via two steps. I don't know why they bothered me. I felt like I was entering a lair within a lair. It was winter and she was sitting next to a fireplace. I thought it ridiculous to have a fire in Miami, but I kept that to myself.

"Hello, George. I have heard a lot of good things about you." She got up and met me half way. I was looking around to see where I should sit.

"Hello, Ms. Blanco," I said. I was determined to keep this formal and professional as I shook her hand.

"Please, Griselda."

She pulled my hand towards her and embraced me. I waited for the pain of the knife to register, but it never did. I wasn't ready for this. Between South American men, I could expect a hug or even a kiss on the neck, but women wouldn't cross those boundaries on a first encounter. It wasn't done. But then again, there weren't many women like Griselda.

She sat and indicated for me to sit next to her. We both had comfortable overstuffed leather armchairs. There was a bowl of fruit between us and a man appeared with a bottle of champagne. I nodded when I saw she was having a drink. We toasted and took a first sip. I looked to see where Jon was. I couldn't find him.

"Are you nervous?" She looked at me with a small smile. She was more attractive than I had expected. Her face was beginning to become round, but there was still a hint of the beautiful woman she once was. I reminded myself not to be fooled. She wasn't known as *La Madrina*—the Black Widow—for nothing.

"To be honest, Griselda, yes. I'm sure it'll pass."

"It will." She reached over and put a hand on mine. I was pleased I didn't flinch; that would have been the end of me.

"First, I would like to thank you for choosing me," I said. "I'm sure you had your choice of anyone in the market."

"Oh, that. Those cocksuckers think they're something just because they have offices in fancy glass buildings. I've moved enough through them. I chose you because of your reputation."

"Reputation? I'm as square as they come."

She smiled and finished her drink. The man returned and filled both our glasses. "Which is why you are perfect. You are young, ambitious, and already know what it takes to move this much product." She watched me as she spoke. I began to think this was her attempt at seducing me. It made me uncomfortable. "Jon told me about your work with the CIA and how it ended."

"I never confirmed anything. You know I can't."

"Even between friends?"

"Especially between friends. If you're right, then I'm the right guy for you."

"And if I'm wrong, you're a dead man. But you know that."

I felt a familiar sour taste in my mouth. It was the same when I met with the generals near the end. Their power was at its zenith and it was never a certainty that you would walk away alive when you met. She exuded the same energy.

"Like you said, I'm too ambitious to be stupid. If I were the wrong man, I'd already be dead."

She laughed. "Enough of this talk. Jon has told me you are able to increase your capacity to meet our demand."

"Of course. I will need to add some procedural elements to the equation, but that isn't your concern. You want your money available to you. I will deliver it. However, there is one issue."

"And that is?" Her eyebrows raised.

"If we are talking about this amount of cash, then we may want to start shipping it to different depositing centers. I don't have that capacity."

"Like you said, that's not my problem." She sat back.

"True, but if you want to extend your operations, you need to survive the scrutiny of the feds. They aren't here yet, but they will be. It's like a war out here. They won't condone this indefinitely."

"They're on the payroll, don't worry."

"With respect, Griselda, they'll bring people in from up north."

She lit a cigarette and inhaled deeply. "Well, that is my problem. We each have matters to attend to if we want to be successful. I have my techniques, you have yours."

I shuddered involuntarily. She had introduced motorcycle assassinations and drive-by shootings to Miami. Looking into her eyes, I believed that the stories were true—she had killed by her own hand. Certainly, she had ordered others to do so.

"That is your business. I am just a simple banker. I'll make sure your cash gets into the system."

"Minus your commission."

"Of course," I said. "But, most importantly, you have complete control. Which leads to my next point."

She didn't say anything. She was smoking and looking at me from the corners of her eyes. I think she was trying to look sexy.

"If this is going to benefit you, we need to begin preparation for a time when these operations end."

She leaned forward. I knew it was always dangerous to talk truth to power, but I gambled that she was more interested in keeping her position than feigning contempt.

"If you get arrested, or the laws change, you don't want the government taking your assets. They need to confiscate some, but I suggest you make the rest impossible for them to reach."

"Isn't that what I pay you for?"

"You pay me to get the cash into the banking system. Paper into ledger entries. The government can still track and seize."

"Is it possible to be truly safe?" She said it with humor, as if the idea of safety was impossible to comprehend. I realized that she had probably never felt safe her entire life. It is how she came to be the monster she was.

"We can try."

Her response startled me. She leaned forward and put her hand on my leg. Her black hair was long and flowing past her shoulders, her lips painted red against a pale face. "We can try later. I want to get to know you better first. Would you like that?"

I looked for Jon. I imagined him howling with laughter at me. I decided I had no choice.

"Of course, Griselda."

∞

"How was your date?" Jon hadn't shaved for a few days and his beard was thick and black. I could see his teeth behind it.

"You knew that was going to happen?"

"You never know anything with Griselda. I suspected. She is voracious in everything. Food, drugs, men, women—everything."

"Women?"

"She's messed up. I've heard of parties where she would pull a gun on a man or woman or both and force them to have sex together or with her. She seems to like men and women equally."

"At least she doesn't discriminate," I said. I wanted to make light of things. The whole event was disturbing. She was about to move twenty million dollars a month through my bank and all she wanted to do is sleep with me. Either she was incredibly lonely or… a thought entered my mind. Or she was lying. I kept my concerns to myself. Her actions will make clear her intentions in due course. Warning bells began to sound in my head.

"You coming to the house with me?"

"Toni?"

"Yeah. She's putting on a party. All the usual people. Come along. We'll try not to infect you."

"I'm trying to be paranoid so that you guys have something if the shit hits the fan. And believe me, it always hits the fan."

"You don't want to be arrested?"

"No. It would be disastrous to you if I did. You would lose your advantages of having me. We need to determine a way to ensure we meet as infrequently as possible."

"I don't have a problem with that," Jon said. "But we are still customers and we have needs."

"Of course." I smiled. "And you will be given every accommodation. The key is to think of things in terms of inside the US and outside the US. Right now, as long as we can get the money into the US banking system and then into the international banking system, you will be fine. We can route the funds into various havens that will protect you, or at least provide enough time to move the funds if you get in danger."

"Like you did for Uncle Sam?"

I extended my hand but said nothing. We shook. "Looks like another perfect Miami day. Blue sky, blue water, beautiful women."

"George, it's too bad you can't join us. You'd enjoy yourself. Why have all this money if you can't enjoy what it buys?"

"I tried that once. It backfired on me."

"Maybe you didn't try hard enough. I've got some girls that'll blow your mind, and the drugs are the best in the world." He took out a cylinder and tapped some cocaine onto his left hand. He sniffed it into his left nostril. He repeated and sniffed into his right nostril. "I could never handle booze, but this stuff is the shit. I can't get enough. Want some?"

I shook my head, then thought better of it. "Okay, just a bit."

He handed me his cylinder and I copied what he did—only with less. It took a few seconds, but my sight became clearer. I felt as though, until then, I had been living with a film over me and now it was off. Within a minute, my lower back was no longer bothering me.

"This stuff is amazing," I said.

"First time?"

"Yeah. I've never been into this before. I was around heroin but I didn't like what it did to people. I puffed a little weed, but none of it stuck."

"Coke'll blow your mind. You should see what happens when you smoke it. I mix it with my tobacco and add horse tranquilizers."

I sat back in my seat and enjoyed the world around me. I felt like I had been watching silent black and white movies and now, everything was in full surround-sound with technicolor. It was sensory overload.

Jon drove at his usual breakneck pace and we were at his home before I realized he wasn't taking me to the airport.

"Thought you might make an exception this one time," he said. His smile was wide and he was into party mode. I already knew he was pretty fun to be around.

I followed him into his house. The whole compound consisted of four houses that I could see, some stables for horses, and a fair amount of land. No one gave me a second glance as I walked with Jon except for a large dog. It ran at us with a predatory zeal.

"Don't move," Jon said.

I stopped dead in my tracks.

"She is very protective. Don't raise your voice or hands."

"What'll she do?"

"She'll attack, rip your throat out, and then make your bowels her meal."

I thought he was exaggerating, but I had no intention of finding out. I had no idea of what breed it was, but it looked like a fighting dog. The ears and tail were cut off. It had short hair with wrinkly skin to prevent bite marks. It must have weighed a hundred and fifty pounds.

"Good girl, Shooter. This is my friend. George, don't move."

I wasn't afraid of dogs; I was afraid of Jon and his reputation. So far, I had only seen the fun side, but I knew his dog didn't have the same mental detachment that he had. She accepted some rough pets and pats from Jon before examining me. She came right up to me, sniffing my feet, then pants, then crotch. I held my hands loosely at my side. I felt her cold nose and bristles of her muzzle as she brushed up against me. She pushed her body against me in an ultimate move of dominance. Satisfied I wasn't a threat, she returned to Jon's side and I walked a step behind.

"I trained her to sniff gun oil. It surprises the hell out of guys when she pins them to a wall. I don't like guys packing heat near me." He reached down and gave a pat to Shooter's chest. It sounded like a muffled drum. There was no fat on this killer.

"Quite the dog."

"She does her job. I'll be putting her in the kennel when the party starts. People get nervous around her."

"I don't know why," I said.

"Exactly."

Once Shooter had been safely put in her kennel, I was met by Toni. She was shorter than Jon, around five foot five, but was a stunner. She looked like she could have been a Bond girl. Her eyes were light green and her hair dark blonde. Behind the glamor shone a fire, and I could understand why he was with her. Somehow, despite the fire, she looked innocent of his activities. She was a distraction for him. I began to see the motivation behind his riches.

"Hello, George. Jon has been telling me so much about you."

"Don't believe everything he says," I joked.

"Do you want a tour of the place?" She ignored my deflection and I began to think that she wasn't so innocent. She didn't want to know, whatever her suspicions.

"Another time, Toni. George is tired. I think he needs a little pick me up before the people arrive." Jon was walking through the house and I followed. Toni fell back when she realized she wasn't wanted.

We arrived at Jon's office and he closed the door behind us. He went to his desk drawer and produced what looked like a candy or sugar bowl, complete with top. It was fine bone china. He placed it on his desk and took off the top. It was full of white powder. I assumed it was cocaine.

"This is the best shit you're going to get, apart from pharmaceutical grade."

He tipped the bowl over and around a third of its contents poured onto the desk. He took the top card from a pack of playing cards and began creating lines. When he had six, he fished out a silver tube from his desk drawer. He put back four lines, two in each nostril. When he handed the tube to me, I figured I didn't have a choice. I did the other two lines.

"Cigar? I've got the finest Cubans."

He already had two in his hands and was cutting the ends. He handed me one and lit both of them.

"Drink?"

He was operating in fast motion. I felt the glass put into my hand. When I tasted it, I realized it was a very good whiskey.

"Relax. The day is over."

"This is a good cigar." I knew I had to say something. I felt I was hostage to his agenda. I just wish I understood what his plan was.

"There's nothing better than a good cigar and whiskey. The coke is my twist on a classic mix. Some people like to take coffee or chocolate; I like coke. The body is pushed and pulled in different directions. It allows you to take more of everything. Just make sure you don't have an appointment the next day. It's a bitch of a hangover."

The longer I stayed, the more I enjoyed the day. The coke and whiskey dulled my concerns. I was becoming intrigued with the lifestyle. He lived like a prince.

"Can I ask you a question?"

"Sure," he said.

"Do you trust the Colombians?"

"To the extent I can trust anyone, sure. I'm only transport. They deal with distribution once it's here. Now I'm dealing with the cash element with you. I'm just a glorified smuggler. Hardly rocket science."

"You don't think they'll kill you?"

"Why should they? They need me."

"And if things go wrong?"

"Everything always goes wrong. That's life. The guys who survive are the ones who deal with it the best."

"And…"

We were interrupted with a bang on the door. I could see rage flash across Jon's face but the guard at the door looked worried.

"What is it?" Jon asked.

"We have visitors—and not for the party. They look mad. It's about yesterday."

Jon got up and went to his desk. Inside, he pulled out a .45 handgun and put it in his waistband. He went to a cupboard behind his desk and pulled out a shotgun. He loaded it and started walking. I was forgotten.

Against my better judgement, I followed him. All of the guards drew their guns. I could see through the windows that Toni was talking to a short South American man. He had a further six men with guns, mainly MAC-10s. These were fully automatic and shot over a thousand rounds per minute. We had them in Laos.

It was seconds before Jon walked up to the same man. He held the shotgun casually, not pointing it at anyone. He was talking. I couldn't hear what he was saying.

Toni didn't move and I wasn't sure if I was impressed or terrified for her.

Jon became more animated, pointing to the sky, his watch, and his balls. I didn't understand why he did that. The South Americans looked serious. None of them looked afraid. It was like two armies meeting to set terms before a battle. I suddenly became aware of the glass that separated them from me. I'd be dead if bullets started flying.

At that moment, Jon turned and pointed at me. All of the men turned to look at me at the same time. Jon began yelling and pointing at me and I became afraid to move a muscle. I saw him motion for his armed guests to stay where they were. He walked back into the house and down the hallway towards me.

"Everything okay?" As I said it, I wanted to punch myself.

"Just peachy," he said, deadpan. He walked past me and into the office. I realized he was pointing towards his office and not me.

Thirty seconds later, he reappeared, walking fast. I could see powder on his moustache. He was wiping his nose and mouth.

When he was next to the boss of the gang, he handed him a paper. The boss took a while to read it. Jon pointed to something on the paper and then to the sky, and then to his balls again. He shrugged his shoulders and waited.

I no longer felt the whiskey or cocaine. I was stone cold sober from adrenaline. I saw the guards fingering their triggers and raising their weapons slowly. The South Americans weren't doing the same. I realized Jon had ordered a pre-emptive hit. I readied myself to run back to the study and get out of the crossfire.

Jon didn't move his head anymore. He was staring at the man a foot away from him. He no longer talked. What happened next would depend on what that little man from South America did.

I saw him nod. He turned to his men and said something. They lowered their weapons. He shook his head and extended his hand to Jon. They shook. He turned to his men and told them to shoulder their weapons.

And that was it.

The South Americans returned to their two Mercedes. Toni and Jon returned to the main house. His guards remained outside. I hadn't felt this type of tension since Laos.

∞

"That looked serious," I said when Jon had returned us to the study.

"Yeah. They came to kill us." He said it without any emotion. He snorted four more lines, and he was half way through his cigar.

"Any reason?"

"They supplied five hundred kilograms of cocaine and we had to abandon it yesterday. It was a major fuck-up. We lost a plane, they lost their shipment. I just about had my balls blown off."

"You lost a plane?"

"Yeah. We bought a new one for all the new business. They aren't the only fuckers who lost out. Cocksuckers. I don't know what the hell they're so concerned about. We're doing a thousand kilos with them next week. My major concern is that they won't be there when we go to pick it up next week."

"You convinced them that you lost it? How do they know you aren't lying?"

"They don't. They wouldn't, except we had the newspaper report confirming that DEA seized four hundred eighty kilos yesterday. Without that, we'd all be dead. Even if we killed them, they'd send more of their goons until we were dead. Better to make peace. Fighting is the last option; but if you have to fight, kill them all."

"They accepted the newspaper clipping?"

"Yeah. It's the only half-assed objective way of them knowing that we are telling the truth."

"But the discrepancy?"

"The twenty keys? Probably the police pocketing it. They're no babes in the woods either."

I digested that while I smoked my cigar. Jon was a unique person. He was comfortable in a hotel bar with entertainers like Richard Pryor, and happy to do deals with bankers who didn't have offices and worked out of cafés. He was equally capable of standing nose-to-nose with killers in his front yard. I watched him as I smoked, trying to find an element of him that was out of control. He was strangely calm.

Chapter Seven

Sylvia

Miami was intense and I was happy to get out of there alive. If the profits weren't so large, I would have abandoned banking with them altogether. To relax, I decided to return to the one thing that didn't mind whether I was rich or poor, old or young—computers. Banking gave me the excuse to purchase and implement state of the art technology. I decided to go to San Francisco to the West Coast Computer Fair. I felt like I was living through a revolution.

"Are you booked for the Apple presentation? I hear they're bringing out a new version."

I gave the pimply student behind the table my details and I got a badge with my name on it. I paid for a program and picked up sheets showing faces I had only read about.

"Yep. That, the Commodore PET, and the other personal computers. I can't believe how this has taken off." I wanted to get inside and wander around the roughly two hundred stalls. Everyone was there: Intel, Digital Research, Apple, IBM. It was a who's who of computing.

I arrived as the doors opened, but I wasn't the only one. There seemed to be thousands who had the same idea. It took almost half an hour before I was able to pay for my ticket, get my badge, and go inside.

The fair didn't disappoint. It was a sea of nerds, tables, and cables. I loved it. I began to wish I pursued this instead of banking. I chose money over what I loved. Hopefully, I would be able to return to this before I missed all of the fun.

"You look like you're afraid to dive in," a voice said next to me. It was a girl's voice. I turned my head.

"Are you talking to me?"

"You, me, everyone. Doesn't matter. You look the way I'm feeling. The words came out."

She was young, probably around eighteen, maybe younger. She had long, blue-black hair and looked out of place in her tailored clothing. The auditorium was full of scruffy geeks like me, just twenty years younger. Their idea of tailoring was Levi jeans and a clean t-shirt.

"You study computers?"

"They don't teach it in class yet. At least, not where I'm from."

"Where's that?"

"Montreal."

"Isn't that the French part of Canada?"

"Yeah, but I don't speak it. Try German, Greek or Latin, and some Spanish. I know, it doesn't make sense. I'll need to learn it at some point."

"Computers?"

"French." She smiled and I could see she came from money. Everything about her was refined.

It wasn't cool to talk to teenagers, but she seemed like an old soul; she just happened to be young at the moment. "Are you looking to buy a computer?"

"Keen on the technology aspect. I love art. From what I read, computing is the future. I'm trying to decide how it will affect art."

"It'll be a long time before computers can do anything more than calculate and perform basic functions. We're a long way from the Jetsons," I said.

"I'm more interested in how museums and governments will utilize computers." She was gazing into the room and people were bumping into us. We were blocking the stream. I motioned with my head to move closer to the wall.

"In what way?" I was surprised at her focus. It was so practical.

"Oh, I don't know. Security, freedom, 1984-stuff."

"You don't look like a hacker."

"Neither do you. Are you a salesman? Opening a franchise?"

I was surprised with her assessment. Normally, I wouldn't care, but I was a Harvard MBA graduate. I was a vet. I was the owner of a bank. I grabbed the last one.

"I own a bank and wanted to see what technology was available. I still use the IBM 5100 but was hoping to see something new. I understand that they have an encryption machine on display here." I felt like I was interviewing for a job. The girl was twenty years younger, yet her eyes hypnotized me. She understood everything and could probably teach me a thing or two.

"Sounds like you have it all figured out." She wore a different type of smirk. It made her mischievous. Was she flirting with me?

"I have applications for the technology. For me, it's not theoretical."

"You hiring?"

The question caught me by surprise.

"Maybe. For the right people."

"I'm the right person for your bank. I will also be able to make your system hack-proof. That's the biggest threat to institutions. Any person with half a brain can walk through the factory default settings on these things."

"And you would know that how?"

"Like I said, I'm the right person for you. I know these things."

"How?"

"It comes easily to me. My parents wanted to keep me challenged, so they arranged to get me some time on the university's computer. I learned Fortran and Basic and loved it."

"University's computer? You seem a little young for that."

"I finished high school early and my father is a professor of literature."

I could see that she wasn't intimidated by older people. She must have been dealing with them her entire life.

"And now you want to go into banking?"

"Never!" She laughed when she realized she had shouted. She covered her mouth, and I saw her face redden. It made her cheeks red and her eyes sparkle when she looked at me. I felt a pang when our eyes connected. "Sorry, I didn't mean to sound like that. Perhaps I meant to say that I would be a consultant rather than an employee. I have a lot of projects that keep me busy. I don't want to be tied down to a job."

"Any job would be full time. It wouldn't be a hobby."

"You don't need me full time. I'm not a receptionist or bank teller. I want to deal with your computers only. I would access it remotely and control it from my home office."

"Home office? You wouldn't work in my office?"

"Only when necessary. Sometimes the tapes or wires need adjusting."

"I think we're a little ways off from that type of employment. I know a thing or two about computers, myself. We couldn't get the data down the wire fast enough to make that practical."

"Possibly, but you need to know what can be hacked and what can't. By operating from my own office, I can tell you that."

"I'm not interested in funding your hacking skills, uh… Sorry, what's your name?"

"Sylvia Öst. Yours?"

"George Anderson. Nice to meet you." I felt her hand in mine and noticed her manicured nails. Her fingers were like silk, smooth and strong. She was feminine and confident.

"And you. I'm sorry, I'm getting carried away. I keep thinking about how I want to lead my life and to find jobs that will promote that. I don't want to shackle myself to a future that isn't flexible, however much I love it. I want to pursue art, travel to Paris on a whim, or New York for the day."

"You want it all," I said. I was beginning to admire her spunk.

"Don't you?" She looked at me and didn't blink.

I became conscious of my need to swallow. "I did. I don't know if it is possible anymore."

Her head turned slightly. The effect was powerful on me.

"Bad experiences?"

"I trusted and believed in the wrong people."

"Ah." It looked like she wanted to say more, but pressed her lips together firmly instead.

I became conscious of the noise of the people around us and blinked like I had been in a dream. "Shall we?"

"In case we get separated during the day, do you want to meet up for dinner tonight? Say, eight o'clock?" She reached into her pocket and pulled out a card. "This is my answering service. If you need to cancel or change, call them and they'll be in touch with me."

I took the card and tried not to laugh. A teenager with an answering service. What rabbit hole had I fallen into? I thought about me at her age and I remembered Barbie and the disastrous planned meeting. Then I thought about Jasmine and how she set me up from the moment we met. Nothing was an accident. There were no coincidences when you go high enough. Was Sylvia another Jas? I looked at the card and shook my head. I decided to meet with her and find out. Whoever she was, I was drawn to her.

"Sounds great. Let's try not to get separated." I almost reached for her hand but stopped myself. She was elegant in her long white coat. It was either cashmere or wool, and definitely expensive. It would be hot with it on. I expected to be carrying it before long. I also began to wonder what she had on underneath.

∞

The day was better than I could have hoped. I never thought about Jon, Griselda, or the bank. While Jas and Barbie drifted initially into my thoughts, they were chased away by Sylvia's savage curiosity. She would be commenting on the process of creating a motherboard one moment, then enjoying the tactile experience of the circuitry against her fingers. She liked the process of everything. She was almost indifferent to the actions or abilities of the various programs and circuitry. She wanted to make it, or at least know how it was made. As a woman, she was given additional attention when they realized she knew what she was talking about. I enjoyed watching tongue-tied virgins stumble over their sales pitch. When she handed me her overcoat, I realized I was in trouble. Her body was like a single stroke on a painter's canvas. It was continuous from the souls of her feet to her crown. She was made of lines that moved together seamlessly. Her dress was modest yet complemented her body.

"I hope you enjoyed today as much as I did," I said. I lifted a glass of local wine. It wasn't very good, but I wasn't going to let bad wine ruin our date. Or was it a meeting?

"I feel energized," she said. Her eyes danced. "Everything seems possible; I want to learn it all."

"You don't need to know everything."

"If I want to protect your bank, I'd better. Remember, there are a lot of people out there who will break into it just as a prank. Once your customers learn of it, they'll run for the hills."

I thought about Jon and the MAC-10s his business partners carried. I shuddered. Some pre-pubescent kid could take a drug lord's money. I would end up skinned and fed to Jon's dog.

"You think it's likely? There aren't that many computers on the market yet."

"Did you see that place today? There will be. Apple is making a great product. IBM will need to reduce its prices or be wiped out. I know my Dad'll buy me one of them."

"For you or him?"

"Hopefully both, but I want something more powerful. I'll probably design my own motherboard and make something that isn't available. If Dad wants to buy me an Apple, I'll ask him to give me the money instead and I'll use the funds to buy parts and build my own."

"You are something," I said. "What do you do for fun?"

"I learn."

"I mean, other than learning."

She leaned in and waited. I leaned in as well. She looked to her left, then right. "Other than sex?"

My mouth went dry and I didn't break her stare. I felt my heart beating and palms begin to sweat. How was this girl doing this to me?

"Uh, yes."

She leaned back and rolled her neck before taking a drink of wine. "Meeting interesting people. Going to fairs like today's. I love wandering through museums. Actually, now that I think about it, I enjoy copying things. That's why I want to know how everything is made. It makes it easier for me to copy it."

"Art?"

"Art, documents, hacking. You name it. I like to know how things work. Then I try to replicate it. After I've done that, I lose interest."

"And you're happy? Some of your interests aren't cheap. Don't you want money?"

Her hair reflected the light of the restaurant. She wore little makeup and seemed comfortable in her skin.

"Money will come." She believed it. There was no doubt.

"From jobs?"

"Sort of. I'll tell you more when I get to know you better."

Our meals arrived and I welcomed the break in intensity. I was almost twice her age, yet she dominated the conversation, the space, and the topics. I had never met someone like her before. I had no doubt what she meant when she said she would get to know me better. I took a bite of my steak and chewed.

The next morning, I felt the ripple of my covers as she left the bed. I turned over and watched her disappear into the bathroom. Am I out of my mind? She's barely legal, and I just met her. *Get control of yourself, George. You've seen this many times. Don't be a victim.*

"You up for breakfast or just coffee?" I said.

Silence. Then I heard the shower. She probably didn't hear me. I picked up the phone and ordered two breakfasts—one standard eggs with bacon, the other solely fruit. I had no idea what she liked. I also ordered lots of coffee. I was gambling that she wasn't into tea. I put my robe on and paced the room. I didn't feel comfortable entering the bathroom despite what we did last night. I needed reassurance that this wasn't a mistake.

The sound of the bathroom door opening caused me to turn around. She wore a towel wrapped around her body that made her previous night's dress look shabby. Her raven hair lay wet against her skin and towel. Her face was fresh with sleep and a hot shower. She smiled and I found myself smiling back. I couldn't believe she wasn't older.

"It's all yours. Great shower."

"Thanks. I ordered breakfast. I didn't know what you prefer."

"I eat everything."

As I walked past, she tiptoed next to me and planted a kiss on my cheek. I wanted to remove the towel but I was becoming wary of her. She was too perfect. I needed to check her out before I allowed myself to get involved.

She was right about the shower. It shook out any cobwebs I had and reinvigorated me.

I had taken a good suite, one with a large lounge in addition to the sleeping area. I found her sitting next to the window, reading the morning paper. If she had any anxiety or concerns, I didn't see it. It unnerved me.

"The breakfasts came. I ate the eggs and bacon. I hope you don't mind."

"Not at all. I just wanted the coffee and some toast. My first major meal is at noon."

"Do you need to talk about last night?" she asked.

I paused. Isn't this the question I was supposed to ask? "Not really. Unless you need to."

"I hate that shit. I like you. You like me. We had fun. That's enough for me. I don't expect it to happen again but would love it if it did."

I looked at her with kaleidoscopic eyes. Each time she spoke, she appeared different to me. At times, irresistible; others, merely odd. I liked not knowing what she was going to say or do. I was beginning to like her.

"It's a date. I'll let you know next time I'm in Montreal."

"I thought you're hiring me."

"I thought you were working from home."

"You and I both know that's bullshit. If you want something to get done, you need to be on the ground." She looked at me and I must have looked like my jaw was going to drop. "Are you okay?"

"Uh, yeah. I can't understand how you aren't pursuing further study. Why work at a microscopic bank when you can make a difference at some university?"

"How? Write a paper? Get graded by teachers who are too burned out to care? Or who want to get me in the sack if I want to get my 'A'? I learned long ago that the only way for me to learn what I needed to know was for me to go out and grab it. I need to learn what your bank can teach me. It would be a win-win." She took a sip of her coffee.

"Sounds good to me. We're based in Montserrat, with correspondent offices in Miami and New York. We only have a small client base and our primary concern is dealing with deposits."

She looked at me carefully as she finished her coffee, not saying anything. She began to chuckle.

"What's so funny?" I asked.

"I was thinking that it would be funny if you were laundering money for bad guys. Even the way you describe your bank sounds fake. I'm sorry. I'm just being an idiot."

I watched her, wondering whether this was a sting. As I watched her, doing nothing, she stopped laughing.

"Holy shit. Don't tell me that's what you're doing. You need to get a better game face, man."

"I didn't say anything."

"You don't need to. I'll tell you one thing: You're not a very good liar."

"You have the wrong idea of what's going on," I said, "but if that's what you think, you probably aren't looking for a job with me."

"Are you kidding?" She sat forward. Her towel became loose and began to fall. She deftly tucked it back in. "Now I really want to join. This is the type of work

I'm interested in. We'll be at the cutting edge of legality, technology, and business."

"Sylvia, you're imagining things. I was watching your towel, not your fantasy about my bank. I couldn't talk because all I could think about was what was underneath."

She smiled and stood up. She shuffled next to me in her slippers, let her towel drop and sat demurely on my lap, looking at me like a puppy. "Is this what you want to see?" She batted her eyelashes and pouted her lips.

I was being played, but I wasn't complaining. I kissed her and she leaned in to whisper in my ear. "I'm the best damn counterfeiter you'll come across. I'm going to be the best in the world. It's all art and I love it. It's my passion. Your business is just the conversion of art into electrons. You need to make sure they're both accepted. I can do that for you."

She had her hands linked behind my neck and was leaning back. She lifted one leg up and around so that she straddled me. I was amazed that she was able to do this with her arms where they were. She was unlike anyone I had ever met. I prayed she was half as good as she thought she was.

Chapter Eight

Laundering

"The Bank Secrecy Act makes it difficult for you to achieve what you want to do. As a bank, you don't need to report cash deposits of less than ten thousand dollars, but you do need to report suspicious activity. This includes depositing lots of sub-ten thousand dollar amounts either in the same branch or across the country. If the bank discovers this, they need to report it. Otherwise, they are breaking the law. The government makes the banks responsible. It then lets the system regulate itself."

Sylvia was pacing in our new office. She insisted that it be swept for listening devices before she talked. She added a regular bug-sweep as a pre-requisite before any major meeting and to sweep at least weekly. The same applied to my home and for the head office.

"It's based on the premise that they make it difficult to get into the system. However, once you are in, things are fairly unregulated—at least so far."

"I understand," I said. "When I started, I didn't imagine any client would have such a high demand for this. I also didn't think anyone would trust me enough to take their money in this quantity." I was amazed at how she had absorbed the books on banking I gave her—and how she broke down the issues into bite-sized pieces.

"But you have this problem and it is up to us to solve it. The big question is whether the correspondent bank has any reason to doubt your integrity. Initially, it won't take any notice. You're too small. A million bucks in cash is a lot of money, but it is nothing to them. Over a month, this represents one hundred deposits of ten thousand dollars. The question is why."

"I know. We have no legitimate reason for this."

"Who says you don't?"

"Our clients are handing us bundles of cash. They aren't normal businessmen."

"Why not?" she said. "This may be simplicity itself. I need to create a profile of hundreds, possibly thousands, of small entrepreneurs who do everything from running restaurants, bowling alleys, and nightclubs to building contractors. Cash isn't illegal yet. It's a nuisance for the government, but someone has to deal with it."

"You're suggesting we create back stories for each deposit," I said. "This way, we can regularize them. Keep it under ten grand, deposit multiple times per week under that alias. We then tie up the cash under the real account once it is in the system. It's like breaking into a bank where there are no guards to worry about—provided you never leave."

"The big banks don't care about the law, except to the extent that they can live within it. So long as we don't rub their faces in it, they won't care. They'll take their transaction charges, correspondence charges, and any other charges they can think up. We'll pass on the charges to the clients and no one will care. It is all about being a chameleon. Our advantage is that we don't need to have huge numbers of shareholders or employees or outside depositors. We just need to look like we do. That's art. That's my specialty." She twirled and bowed with a flourish.

"At some point we'll need to eliminate the correspondent bank. It is our weakest link."

"I agree, but let's walk before we can run."

I was being lectured by Sylvia on things I had already learned in Harvard. I held my tongue. I had dealt with lunatic Laotian generals, CIA top brass, and actual drug lords, but Sylvia lectured me as though I barely knew anything.

"I've been thinking," she said. "If these numbers are anything to go by, then we are about to see the biggest transfer of money and influence the world has ever seen."

"I don't know if I'd go that far," I said. Every once and a while, she would say something that reminded me of how young she was.

"It has to be. The mafia made its money running booze during the prohibition, but they don't touch drugs. They have the infrastructure in place for influence and power, yet have turned their back on the biggest profit opportunity of the last two centuries. If the US government doesn't stop the Colombians, they'll make more money in the next decade than the mafia has made in the last century."

"From your lips to God's ears," I said. "Which means we need to create entire communities of false people to assist us."

"Which means we need to do this so perfectly or we're both dead."

"You wanted a challenge."

"I think I've just gone from employee to silent partner."

I didn't say anything. I feared she was right.

∞

Sylvia and I began to create a fantasy infrastructure and I was glad we had computers to keep track of everything. I didn't want to trust her on this, but I had no choice. I ensured that we didn't trust anyone else. If we got it right, we would generate riches beyond our wildest imagination. I began to believe that I would generate a pool of wealth even larger than that taken from me by the CIA.

"Any requests for information?"

"None," I said. "Bank of America has accepted all of our deposits without a hiccup. I've pooled everything and our next step is to wire it to Montserrat. This will be our first ten million dollars of deposits."

"Do they want it taken out in Montserrat?"

"I'll do whatever they want," I said. "It's their money. If I were them, I'd leave it in the financial system. I don't know any other way for them to launder it so inexpensively. The usual way is to create fronts— nightclubs, cash businesses. We are able to have all the benefit without the aggravation of actually running businesses."

"We need to be careful." Sylvia was stretching. Neither of us had a full night's sleep for months. "At some point, we'll need to shut down these accounts. The IRS will do spot audits and we'll be finished."

"Let's jump off that bridge when we get there," I replied. "One step at a time."

Sylvia closed the door to my office and locked it. She walked to the windows and drew the curtains. When she returned to face me, she locked her eyes on me and began undressing.

"Isn't this what it's all for?" she said. She undressed slowly, allowing each button to last seconds.

"Happiness?"

"Sex."

"I think we want more from life than just sex, don't you think?" I loved that we would talk like this, even at a moment like this. She was the whole package—mind and body. Each part complemented the other, making each stronger.

"You're debating me on the merits of getting rich?"

"No, just what it is to be rich."

She stopped undressing and sat on my lap. Her fingers found their way into my hair.

"To get rich, you need to want to be rich. That's the step most people never take," she said. "Then, you need to figure out what it means to be rich for you. Each person is different. For me, it means pursuing my art without hindrance. To achieve that, I need a lot of money."

"For me, to be rich is to be free," I said. "Growing up, money was the gatekeeper to my dreams and ambitions. I would think, if only I had more money, I could go to this school, have that girlfriend, or go on this holiday. I didn't worry about material things. In my mind, I had enough. I wanted the experiences that would make me happy, and those things cost money." I didn't add that the only experience I ever wanted was for Barbie to love me and marry me. Any amount of money I would make now could never make that happen. Money can't turn back the clock.

Sylvia saw my eyes glaze over. "Where are you?" She had stopped trying to be sexy. The mood was gone. Perhaps Fleetwood Mac was right—rulers don't make good lovers.

"Ancient history." I tried to stand, but she was still on my lap. She got off.

"Who was she?"

Damn, this woman is sharp, I thought.

"She broke my heart."

Sylvia put her hand on my face and looked like nothing I had seen before. There was a softness and vulnerability deep within her.

"I wish someone would hurt me like that," she said.

I put my hand on her face and we stood there for a moment before I leaned in. She kissed me, and I was overwhelmed by the feelings she stirred within me. We made love like people adrift, terrified to let go of each other. I felt her cry softly afterwards.

∞

By the time Ronald Reagan was elected president, my bank had moved over two hundred million dollars. My cut was five percent. I made sure I took some of that and put it away, just in case. I didn't want to be left holding the bag if this venture went pear-shaped.

"Lending rates are over twenty-two percent and inflation is over thirteen percent," I said. "If we don't start lending this money out, all our efforts will have been wasted."

"What do you mean? We're moving almost a hundred million a month in product. The Colombians are ready to increase their deposits into your bank to thirty million per month. Who cares about inflation?" Jon was relaxed. We were on his boat, ostensibly fishing, away from any ears.

"For every one hundred bucks you have today, you will have only eighty-five bucks this time next year. That's why."

"Buy T-bills. They're running at inflation. Problem solved."

It was disarmingly simple. I wanted to make a business from all the capital they had accumulated. They wanted liquidity. I realized that they never planned past tomorrow. Why should they? They might be dead.

"And they'll be happy with that?"

"Bro, they're over the moon. They'll probably never need the money you're holding. You're not the only bank they're using."

"Fair enough. As long as they know what they want, I'll do it. We've got something special going on here. We're creating a wealth base that the politicians and lawmakers won't be able to touch."

Jon leaned forward. "Don't believe it. If those cocksuckers smelled free money, they'll steal it in a heartbeat. Don't put your head above the parapet. It'll just get shot off."

I forgot who the more street-wise criminal was. I should have known that the rules I grew up with and learned in Harvard no longer applied. I had firmly and resolutely crossed the line. I couldn't rationalize that I was merely facilitating clients. I was a criminal because I aided and abetted criminals. I made a profit ensuring that the government didn't receive its taxes on the laundered money. I was working on a way to ensure that the government couldn't trace the deposits and seize them.

"You don't want me to do anything with the money? There are a lot of opportunities to leverage this into something very big. We are big enough to buy American banks. We can buy one of the thrifts, or even an investment bank. We are talking about a lot of money on deposit."

"George, relax. We're all rich. Enjoy it. Having a hundred more toilets doesn't mean you're gonna shit any better."

I laughed despite myself. "You've got a way with words. I don't agree, but I'll follow your instructions."

"Hey, listen. I'm not the one in charge. I'm just telling you what they will say. If you want to ask them yourself, go ahead."

"I'm shit-scared of Griselda. I'd either get raped or killed or both."

"I'm not judging her, bro. She's a powerful woman. More powerful than any of the Guido's in Jersey or New York, that's for sure. But she's only one finger in the fist. I'm talking about the real bosses in Colombia."

I wondered why they still needed me. I guess I was white and it was easier to keep the status quo. Or I haven't given them an excuse to kill me.

Yet.

"Okay, you're the boss."

"No, just the best goddamn smuggler you'll ever meet."

I checked my line. No bites. Neither of us cared. Jon was jacked up on coke, and I was chilling with my cigars and scotch. Maybe he was right. Maybe it was time for me to enjoy myself. If all went well, my bank would have a couple of billion dollars in deposits earning just over twelve percent on T-bills. Five percent of that wasn't bad. I could afford to be happy.

∞

I returned to New York expecting to find Sylvia in her apartment. She wasn't there. I called her answering service and waited for her to get in touch. We had been together long enough to know that we should be together forever. I wanted to know that she was mine. I went to my apartment while I waited.

I had purchased an even more luxurious apartment to replace the one seized by Jasmine and the CIA. It was over four thousand square feet and boasted some of the richest, most powerful people in the world as neighbors. I was pleased with my purchase. I nodded to the doorman, then the porter, as I walked into the skyscraper apartment block. The gold leaf, brass, and marble didn't look ostentatious anymore. It was home.

It signaled comfort and security. I was safe when I opened those doors.

As the elevator doors closed behind me, I walked the few steps to the secure door into the apartment. Many residents liked the idea of the elevator being able to open into their apartment. I felt it was too much of a security risk.

The door was heavy and I felt as much as smelled the familiar air of my home when I was inside.

"George!"

I spun around to see Sylvia. She was surprised to see me.

"Sylvia. I've been trying to contact you."

She came towards me.

"Sylvie! Where are you?" Her eyes, then head, turned to follow the voice. I followed her eyes and saw a woman coming out of my bedroom. She was naked.

The room fell silent. I looked at the two of them. I blinked, trying to take in what I was seeing.

"I thought you loved me," I said. It sounded so pathetic.

"I do." She closed the distance between us. "I just don't feel like you love me."

"You know I do."

"In my mind, yes. But my body doesn't feel it."

She had her hands on me and my body was reacting to her touch. Her words hurt. I thought I was a good partner, an attentive lover. A future husband.

"So you went to the other side?" I raised my eyebrows at the guest.

"It's not what it looks like."

"It's pretty hard to get this picture wrong." I took a step back and removed her hands from me.

"Gina is a good friend. It's fun."

"Is she the only one?"

"You mean you haven't been with other women?"

"No." The word was short and punctuated the increasing tension in the room. Gina hadn't moved. "Neither have I been with other men," I added. I wanted to ensure that I got my point across.

"I'm sorry, George. I was lonely, and you're gone so often. I needed someone."

"Then get a dog. This isn't on, Sylvia. I'm not like this. I want you as my wife, not part of a harem, and I definitely don't want to be part of yours."

"Wife?" Her eyes watered and I saw the first tears begin. "Why now?"

"I needed time. Funny enough, it took a drug-dealing womanizer to remind me how stupid I've been. I came back determined to marry you."

"George." Her voice was soft. Gina was forgotten and I saw her return to the bedroom as Sylvia came closer to me. "All I ever wanted was to be loved for who I am."

I felt her kisses on me and I wanted to run. My body wanted her.

"I can't do this, Sylvia. I'm not wired like this." I picked up my jacket and walked to the door. "I'll be back in a few hours. Please don't be here."

I rode the elevator down in silence. My eyes refused to focus. I left the building and turned left.

I walked through Central Park, then got bored of all the happy people. I changed direction again. The weather was cool but it wasn't raining. I didn't notice when two kids bumped into me, nor did I hear the barking dog. There were sirens, but there always were. I walked in front of a car and it blared its horn at me. I didn't even turn my head.

The terraced houses that appeared caused me to stop walking. I lost track of time. I turned and saw the house of Barbie's parents. I wasn't planning to come here, but part of me must have. I walked up the stairs, convinced that they would have moved. It was so long ago.

I rang the doorbell and waited.

Chapter Nine

Barbie

"You look well, George." Mrs. Lexington was older but still refined.

"Thank you, Mrs. Lexington. You are looking radiant, as usual."

"Oh, you're such a charmer."

"I'm sorry to drop in on you after all these years," I said. "I was walking and found myself on your street. It seemed like an invisible hand directed me."

"You are always welcome here. You know that." She motioned for me to follow her into the lounge.

"And Mr. Lexington is well, I hope?"

Her faced darkened slightly. "He passed three years ago. Heart attack. It was hard on all of us."

"I'm sorry to hear that. I didn't know." I leaned forward, unsure how I should act.

"There was no way for you to know. I miss him."

"And Barbie?" I asked as casually as I could, but my heart was racing.

"She's got two lovely children. Divorced, unfortunately, but coping well."

"Please send her my regards. I haven't seen or heard from her since, you know, then." All I could think about was that she wasn't married.

"Tell her yourself. She'll be back any time now. She likes to take them for a walk before their nap time."

"Oh," I said. My mouth felt like it had glue in it. "How old are her children?"

"Seven and five. Both boys. Lovely children. I know it isn't under the best of circumstances, but I'm glad to have them around me."

"I'm sure. They say children are the investment and grandchildren are the dividends. You are just reaping what is your due." I had heard it before and thought it was clever. It was the first time I was able to say that nugget in conversation.

Barbie's mother dabbed her eyes lightly and smiled. I took that as a good sign.

I heard the keys in the door and then the sound of children being undressed and straining to be let free. Two streaks of energy burst into the room, immaculately dressed, and jumped into Mrs. Lexington's arms.

"See? They are adorable."

Just as quickly, they disappeared.

"Only one cookie each," a voice called after them. Barbie walked in, flushed and smiling. When her eyes fell on me, her smile froze. "George?"

I stood up. "Barbie."

She came towards me and gave me a kiss on each cheek. "Why are you here? Is everything okay?"

"I was in the area and thought I'd pop in. I'm sorry to hear about your father." I didn't say anything about her divorce.

"Thank you. You are kind to say that."

"I liked him."

"He liked you."

We were silent for a moment as we took each other in.

"I guess I should be going. I don't want to take up too much of your time."

"Will I see you again?" she asked.

"If you want," I said. "I'm in town most of the time. Perhaps we can take in a dinner and a show?"

"Sounds perfect." She was smiling and I remembered why I fell in love with her all those years ago.

I picked her up with a limo from her house and we went to see West Side Story and then had dinner at Bond 45. It wasn't what I had hoped for, but she was happy. We came back to my place for drinks.

"George, your place is amazing!" Her mouth was open as she took in the cityscape below.

"I'm glad you like it."

"Are you going to tell me what you do or keep me guessing?" She allowed me to remove her mink.

"You never asked me."

"I'm asking you now."

"I started a bank. It's doing well."

Her body was fluid and her eyes took in every detail of the apartment. "I knew you would be a success. My father knew it too."

"Then why didn't you meet me at the top of the Empire State building?" I said it before I meant to. I didn't want to fight.

She looked at me and locked my gaze. I could feel tears begin in my eyes. It was a hurt I hadn't felt in decades. She made me feel like it was yesterday. She came next to me and kissed me softly. It was like silk.

"I'm sorry," she said. "I was a fool in a rush to secure my future. I wanted everything the world had to offer. I wanted you but…"

"I didn't have any money," I finished.

She lowered her eyes. "Yes. I'm embarrassed. I acted like a monster and you are treating me like a perfect gentleman."

I wondered if she would be saying the same words if I was broke. I held my tongue.

"We have both moved on. I didn't know about your situation." I didn't say divorce or children.

"He was a bastard. We tried to save the marriage by having children. It wasn't enough."

I wondered what was enough for her.

"And the other guy? The one you left me for?"

"Didn't stick. He was into weird shit."

I didn't comment. My concept of weird was now different than most.

"And the future? Are you working? Seeing anyone?"

"I hope to see you again." She had regained her confidence and allowed her nose to brush against mine. I had a brief image of her as a whore in Laos.

"Drink?" I wanted to put some distance between us. She wasn't the girl I fell in love with. This version was more crass, less happy, and vacuous.

"Champagne, if you have it."

"I do. Coming right up."

I wanted her out of my apartment and out of my life. It was a mistake trying to revisit the past. She was a chimera that had scarred me, and she disgusted me.

"Barbie, I've thought a lot about you over the years."

"Really?" She sipped her bubbles and looked at me over the rim of her glass. I supposed she thought it was sexy.

"I'm really pleased to have bumped into you."

"Me too." She slipped her arm around me.

"It allows me to finally get you off that viewing platform. I have spent countless hours imagining you coming through that elevator door. Instead, you didn't call or write. I was dead to you."

Her arm slipped off my waist.

"You hurt me in ways I am only coming to realize. Seeing you again makes me understand what a monster you had inside of you. Unfortunately for you, that monster has taken you over."

"You bastard," she said. She threw her drink in my face. It felt good.

"I would have made you my Helen of Troy. Instead, you became my Medusa."

She was collecting her coat and reaching for the door.

"Here," I said, throwing some bills towards her. "That's for tonight."

"Asshole," she said, and closed the door.

I felt great.

Chapter Ten

Getting Out

It was awkward for a while with Sylvia, but she and I loved each other too much to let her infidelity ruin our friendship. I wouldn't let her do that to me again, but I loved being around her, and she was the best business partner I could hope for.

"You want to sell?"

"I do," I said.

"While you're making money hand over fist?"

"Absolutely. The DEA and American government are going to get on top of this drug thing sooner or later. If we are anywhere near this, our lives are over. Money won't mean anything. We'll be tainted."

"How do you hope to convince your partners?"

"They're my clients, not partners," I said.

"Same difference with these guys."

"I think there's enough distance between us."

"I'm not convinced," she said.

"If we get out now, can you cover our tracks?"

She smiled. "You know how to sweet-talk a girl, don't you?"

"There's a relatively new bank that Bank of America is in partnership with. I think they may be suitable for our clients. I think the other parties are a Pakistani and a Saudi prince. I know the founder; he's always up for a deal."

"Be careful," she said.

"I just want our heads firmly on our shoulders when we separate from these guys. There's a lot of heat and this needs to be a financial transaction."

"Involving billions of dollars."

"Small potatoes for banks, and we're not announcing anything. We're not looking for publicity." I looked into the middle distance as a memory returned. "That's the name. It finally came to me. Bank of Credit and Commerce International. If you can make our bank disappear from the history books, I'll see if BCCI wants to accept a large deposit. I'll let Jon know about our going out of business and that's it. I've lost the fire for this job."

"I'd like six months to erase our paper trail. Do we have that much time?"

"Reagan will likely be re-elected by then. We have no choice. Let's close this thing down. I'm on the next plane to Miami."

∞

I was nervous going to the meeting. Jon was becoming increasingly crazy, especially now that he was hanging out with the Colombian bosses directly. Each one was crazier than the next. Drugs, sex, and violence. I didn't want to know.

I met him at The Forge, one of his hangouts in Miami. I was escorted to a private room in the back. It looked like the party had already started. He got up and greeted me like a long lost best friend.

"George. Glad you could make it. Come here, you're sitting next to me."

I followed him and took in the scene. The walls were covered with a gaudy gold wallpaper. The floor had an expensive-looking Persian carpet on top of the marble. The table looked antique—dark, solid wood with engravings that someone better than me would recognize. It had a white tablecloth and was covered with open bottles of wine, various finger food, bread, and plates waiting for mains.

"You were late so I ordered you a steak. I hope you don't mind."

I shook my head. There were three other men. One had a stub for an arm and looked mean. The other two looked either Cuban or Colombian. Judging from my company, I assumed Colombian. Next to each man—and me—was a woman, each more beautiful than the next. I was introduced to each man. I couldn't understand the pronunciation of any of their names. I smiled and nodded.

As I sat, Jon pulled out a bag of coke and put it on the table. It was passed around. When it returned, half of it was gone. He set out some lines. He snorted two and indicated me to do the same. I did. Each girl next to us followed suit.

Any nervousness disappeared. The room seemed to focus and I saw Jon pull out another pack of pills. It too went around the table. I saw the guys take a handful and put them in their pockets. They popped one back and made the girls do the same. When it arrived, I raised my eyebrows at Jon.

"Quaaludes. It'll blow your mind. Watch what it does to the girls."

Not taking it wasn't an option. I popped it back and hoped for the best.

The doors opened and the waiters came in with steaks, oysters, crabs, and enough vegetables to choke a horse. Jon gave them a large bill and told them not to return.

I cut into my steak. It was delicious. The girl next to me was half-leaning into me while she ate. I could see that she was becoming overheated. She only ate the oysters and crabs. The next time I looked at her, she had taken her top off. She noticed my glance and looked at me like she wanted to devour me where I sat.

I looked down the table and one of the girls was be-tween the legs of the man with a stub for an arm. The two Colombians were indicating to their girls to do the same. Jon was doing another line of coke from the chest of the girl next to him.

Part of me just wanted to keep eating my steak.

It got crazy when stub-man got up and decided to do a magic trick. It was too late before I realized what he was about to do. He yanked the white tablecloth as fast as he could. Instead of leaving everything where it was, it all crashed to the floor.

Wine was pouring everywhere. He picked up the girl who was between his legs and put her on the table. He stuck one of the bottles of wine into her and emptied it before I turned away, disgusted. I could hear the sound of him grunting like an animal with the girl shortly afterwards.

More coke was snorted and the scene became even more wanton.

One of the Colombians had his girl bent over the table as he took her from behind. He slapped her with steaks, one in each hand. Occasionally, he would take a bite out of one of them. He howled like a wolf. Each person became more feral as the drugs took hold.

I am embarrassed at what I did, for I was no better than the rest. We all descended into an orgy of sex. At one point, all the girls were told to kneel with the asses in the air. We put cherries in their cracks. When we slapped their ass, the cherries flew against the wall. Jon told the girls that he'd give them five hundred bucks for every cherry they caught in their mouth. That entertained us for quite a while.

There were more disgusting things committed that night. I would like to say that it was a blur. It wasn't. It was in full, vibrant technicolor. It was sensational. It was mad. It broke every rule I still held.

When we finished, I was struck at the image of me watching the girls' naked bodies searching for their clothes. Everything was covered in wine, food, and cocaine. At one point, a waiter tried to come in. Jon shot into the air with his gun. Now we had plaster dust on us as well. We took some more cocaine and carried on for another hour before cracking open the door to let in the waiters.

The restaurant was empty, presumably after they heard the gunshots. Jon could barely speak and we all staggered out. He handed the manager a card.

"Call me in the morning. I'll cover all the costs. I'm too messed up right now to talk." Jon's driver popped up from one of the tables to help him walk. He turned to me before he disappeared out the front door. "Come by tomorrow or the next day and we'll talk."

Then he was gone.

I grabbed a taxi and collapsed in my hotel room. I decided I'd call him the day after tomorrow.

∞

Two days later, the sun was shining—it was always shining—and I went to his ranch. It had mosquitoes the size of vampires and I didn't understand why he wanted to be so close to the marshland. His home was almost an hour out of Miami. I found him lounging by the pool, drinking a cola, as though the other night was just another business meeting for him. His girlfriend was inside the house, making lunch.

"So you want to bail on me?"

The question took me by surprise.

"Why the surprise? You've made no secret that you don't want to be seen or associate with me. I figured if you're here, it means you have something to say."

I reminded myself not to underestimate Jon.

"Jon, I don't mean any disrespect. My heart isn't in it anymore. I'm here to ask you how I can walk away."

He looked at me. This time it was his turn to be surprised.

"I have to tip my hat to you. Usually, you cocksucker Harvard fucks—no disrespect intended—are arrogant pricks. You think you have the upper hand and begin dictating terms to us poor ignorance peasants. But today, you impressed me."

I didn't say anything.

"Today, you asked my opinion. I've seen a lot of sticky situations. Ten years ago, I would shoot first and ask questions later. That got me into a lot of trouble. I realized the power of talking when I was forced to ask Meyer Lansky if it was okay for me to kill his stepson. He didn't give a shit about his stepson, but if I had moved against him without permission, Lansky would have to kill me. As it was, he gave me a free pass to kill the little prick."

"What did he do?"

"He shot my partner's brother over an argument of twenty dollars. Shot him in the face like a dog in the bar. The kid died in my partner's arms."

"Shit."

"Yeah. We had to kill the little shit. We would be dead if we killed him without permission—anywhere in the world, Lansky would have found us. But by asking, everyone won."

Except the stepson, I thought.

"So, do you have a solution for me?"

"You've been a good guy, George. I don't know. I've never been in this situation before. If you were to ask me, I would think that any person getting out of this business might be a rat."

"Quitting while you're ahead isn't the same as quitting."

"Good quote. I'll remember that. But our friends are moving upwards of a hundred million a month in product. You have become a valuable tool for them."

"I'm not their only tool. They don't put all of that through my bank."

"For all I know, they may be doing ten times that. This is the amount that runs through my fingers," Jon said.

"I have an alternative bank for them to deal with— if they aren't already dealing with them."

"That's a good start, but that leaves them with the problem of cash."

"They need to be convinced that this avenue is closed. Better to salvage the money they have with the bank now. Transfer it to BCCI—that's the bank I recommend—and find alternative ways to launder the cash. Otherwise, they risk losing the whole shooting match via me. Every penny earned from my bank, if linked to crime, can be seized. There will be nowhere to hide. Better to shut everything down. Then, all the money they have already laundered is safe. That's billions. If it becomes tainted, there isn't a bank in the world that's safe."

"Your argument is good for shutting down your bank, not for you stopping your work with them."

"I'm burned out. I'm of no use to them. Maybe things will change. I'd like to leave a door open, just in case I change my mind."

"I can't speak for them, but I'll make your case the best I can. It will be their decision."

"What does your gut say?"

"I doubt it."

"What should I do?"

"Go back to New York. If you wake up dead, you'll know your answer."

I watched his face to see if he was joking, but only saw his dead eyes.

Chapter Eleven

Change of Plans

When I returned to New York, I woke up the next morning, and the morning after that. I felt grateful for the little things. I gave Jon the details of BCCI and waited to hear whether it would be acceptable to the Colombians. I transferred Sylvia's and my money out. I put her thirty million into Switzerland. I also put my thirty million into Switzerland. I didn't let her know about the other hundred million I put into Liechtenstein and Luxembourg. I couldn't afford to go through this type of experience again if some agency took it all away. I was forty-five years old, and I was done.

Within the month, I received the go-ahead to transfer the funds to BCCI and we officially closed down my bank. IGA Bank of Montserrat was no more. All history of its customers was expunged from our records. As there were no other records than ours, that meant they no longer existed. If there was an investigation, there would be no proof, no paperwork, and no trail. If anything, Bank of America would find itself in trouble for regulatory concerns. I hoped it never came to that.

My parents' portion was part of the Luxembourg payment. I made sure that their farm was fully paid off. Ostensibly, it was for the sale of some land—so he could prove the source of funds to the IRS if anyone asked. I didn't think clearing debt would be so troublesome. I also made sure that they had enough money to live comfortably. They didn't want anything; they told me they were happy with what they had. They were happier knowing I was enjoying my work and being successful. I wished I had their perspective on life. They felt rich with each other. It made me feel poorer than ever.

Sylvia became more interested in counterfeiting. I never understood her fascination. She derived an enormous joy in being able to manipulate paper, government records, and perceptions of people around her. I realized it was her way of bending reality to her will. In her way, she was rich beyond compare.

I took a cruise. I didn't want to be contactable. I disappeared for a year, floating aimlessly with idle rich and retired people. I enjoyed the peace and varied scenery. Then one day, I couldn't distinguish one country from the next, one village from the other, and one day from one month. I decided to return to New York and the land of the living.

The air seemed foreign and the cleanliness annoying. Everything about my apartment building seemed fake. I had someone open the door for me, push the elevator buttons for me, and even carry my luggage. Before my involvement with Jon, I would have called this a blanket of security. I aspired to this life. Now that I had it, it felt vacuous, yet I knew I would never give it up.

My front door was the first familiar thing that made me smile. It was a specialized steel door and was meant to be impregnable. It had oak finishes added to the outside to make it indistinguishable from the others. I loved the sense of safety it gave me. I smiled knowing it would be easier to go through the wall than the door.

The porter put my bags down and I tipped him. It was a long journey that brought me back to the beginning. I walked to the lounge to open the drapes and found them already drawn. I turned to see a person sitting in my favorite chair.

"Hello, George."

She got up and walked towards me. It was dramatic and unexpected. I thought it was a hit. I braced myself for the inevitable bullet but received a kiss instead.

"Hello, Sylvia."

"You look relaxed," she said.

"How'd you get in?"

"You know me. I made an extra key for myself, just in case."

"Remind me to change the locks."

"Don't bother. I have a habit of overcoming things like that."

She looked great. I followed the lines of her tailored outfits to the tips of her fingers. She always flowed and I was endlessly fascinated at how she was put together as a person. Her brain was second to none, and her body could have been an Olympian. I couldn't help but wonder at the marvel of genetics when it all came together in one package.

I tried to be casual about the trespass. It was Sylvia, and I'll always love her. Who wouldn't want to come home to a beautiful woman sitting in their lounge? I went to the bar and pulled out my good scotch, aged fifty years. It was a deep caramel color and I never let people know I had any. It was only for me and, possibly, people like Sylvia.

"I assume this isn't a social call," I said, handing her a glass. Two fingers, neat, just like mine. "Otherwise, you would have rung."

"This is good stuff," she said. She sucked her lips before continuing. "No wonder you hide it."

I lifted my glass in a silent salute.

"I have a problem." She was standing near me again and I could feel a warmth coming off her body.

"Just one?"

"I've got myself mixed up with an older guy. Nothing like that. He's a spook, I think."

"You've been recruited?"

"Not exactly, but not not recruited, if that makes sense."

"It doesn't."

"He's a clever guy and I think you'd like him. I know enough about people not to cross him."

"Who does he work for?" I asked.

"I don't know and he didn't say. If I had to guess, I'd say CIA."

"Why are you telling me?"

"Because you were, or are, CIA." Her eyes were half-closed as she enjoyed the scotch. We had never talked about this and I never told her.

"I'm not CIA."

"George, you forget what my specialty is. I find out things. I know things."

"And?"

"I know a bit more about you now than I did before, and I need someone with your background to give me advice."

"You can't negotiate with the CIA. It's their way or the highway." I returned for a refill.

"Which is why I have to do this."

"Do what?" Finally, she was getting to the point.

"They seem to know things about me. Things that could cause me more than embarrassment. Things that would involve incarceration."

"Like I said, they make you do things."

"They need deniability and they need talent. I have been chosen."

"Damnit, Sylvia. Can't you just tell me what you have to do?"

She looked at me and held out her glass. I splashed some more of my reserve stock into it.

"Nothing less than the downfall of the USSR."

She drank the entire contents, put down the glass, and sat down hard into the sofa. My glass remained halfway towards my mouth. I wasn't sure whether to laugh or throw her out.

"You and which army?"

"That's what's so intriguing. They only need money. Black money, and lots of it. They believe that things are teetering on the edge and all they need to do is help accelerate the rot."

"What the hell are you talking about?" I was tired of the company's mad schemes and the way they would drop me after they tired of me.

"They think they have found a chink in the armor of the USSR. They want to exploit it, the good old-fashioned way."

"Assassination?"

"They have been trying to kill the cat with bombs and bullets. Now, they want to try killing it with cream."

"Sylvia, can you please stop talking in riddles? I know you enjoy this, but I'm tired."

"They want to bankrupt the satellite states of the USSR and leverage the financial instability there to sever them from the evil empire. If all goes well, the lack of confidence will cause the entire rotten USSR to collapse in on itself."

"You want to lend them money?"

"Yes."

"How?"

"That's the tricky part. It can't look as though the US is involved."

"They're enemies, of course they'll be suspected. Besides, why would the satellite states borrow from the US?"

"They won't. They can't. They are supposed to be totally self-sufficient. But they do need some hard currency—that is, not only rubles. They receive dollars from the sale of their oil, which they do at below market rates."

"Great, but I didn't think the satellite states exported oil."

"They don't. They need hard currency from Moscow. They are looking at the GDR, East Germany. It has an increasing standard of living compared to the rest of the USSR and other satellite states. They're also smart. They took western technology and reverse-engineered it."

"What?"

"They bought computers and other shit and figured out how to copy it. Because they could see it worked, they only needed to figure out how to do the same. It is a way engineers copy things."

"Congratulations."

She ignored me.

"They have made a major strategic error and are too stupid to change course."

"Sylvia, I really am not interested in a history lesson."

"This is happening right now. East Germany is making microelectronics, thinking that it can be competitive with the rest of the world. Instead, it's a hundred times more expensive. Their leaders don't want to admit their mistakes and they are building up a foreign debt."

"So they go bankrupt. Big deal."

"I thought you were the big MBA guy from Harvard."

"I'm the realist who says that countries can do things people can't. A person or company goes bust and it's game over; a country goes bust and it prints more money."

"But you forget what happens in the interim. The citizens of that country will be upset."

"So Moscow sends in the tanks, just like it did in Czechoslovakia in '68, Hungary in '56—and the people quiet down."

"Maybe, but the CIA believes there is a chance."

"So they're conducting a financial war against the Russians?"

"Many fronts," she said. Her glass was empty and she went to put in some more. "You want a top-up?"

I nodded.

"Long story short, we are to help East Germany balloon its foreign debt, fund dissidents within the country and all along the other satellite states, and do whatever we can to fan the embers of discontent."

I raised an eyebrow at the word 'we'. She didn't notice and I wanted to get to the bottom of this mad plan; I decided to let it go. "Sounds easy. Why do they need you?"

"Because they can't get the government to openly allocate that amount of money or to attack in that fashion. In case it fails, they don't want to have to answer awkward questions, or worse, be kicked out of office."

"And you have a plan?"

"I do," she smiled. "One as old as time. We create a diversion, a scandal, large enough to encompass the minds of the world's outraged liberals. We allow a few fall-guys to be sacrificed, and our real intention is not even known or discussed."

"How do you plan to pull off something as audacious as this without people knowing or suspecting?"

"Drugs, illegal money, weapons, and enemies with grudges a lot older than ours with the USSR."

"This sounds like it's going to take a while. Can I get washed and eat something?"

Sylvia didn't miss a beat. "Do you want any company?"

I shook my head with a smile and went to my bedroom. As I turned on the shower to warm up the water, I heard the click of the bedroom door closing. I didn't need to crane my neck. Sylvia walked in, already naked.

∞

"You want to risk war in the Middle East and Central America to fan a real war between America and the USSR?"

"Brilliant, isn't it?"

I rolled over and pulled myself up so I was sitting against the headboard. Sylvia did the same.

"You want Israel to sell arms to Iran. The US then sells more arms to Israel, generating money. You want to take that money and give it to the Contras in Nicaragua to fund its civil war against a democratically-elected Sandinista government?"

"Yeah, but with a twist. We've already more-or-less done that to get the release of hostages held in Lebanon."

"We?"

"I like team-talk. Less confusing. We're on the side of the US. We're now a 'we'."

I rolled my eyes. Her youth crept in during times like this.

"As long as we use Israel as an intermediary, we're okay. I want to take this one step further. To make it illegal, the US should sell directly to Iran. It should then use the funds to fund the Contras. The key is that the government must try to keep it a secret, even from President Reagan. It should look like a red-in-tooth move by an out-of-control general. We will have to sacrifice him."

"And all of this is the diversion?"

"That's the beautiful part. While they are looking there, they won't see the wall of money we are moving towards East Germany. You know how much those Colombians make. We know where the bodies are buried. There is a lot of unclaimed drug money sitting in the banking system. We scoop it up, redeploy against our bigger enemy, and hope it all works."

The sheets fell below her breasts and I felt myself stirred by her indifference to her nakedness. Her mind was connecting dots all over the globe, juxtaposing religious hatred with political survival and global thermal nuclear annihilation if it all went wrong. I found her irresistible.

∞

"I can't go back to Jon," I said. "He's gone quiet. The rest are in jail or dead."

"Are the Colombians dead?"

"There's always someone to replace them."

"What about the money we directed to BCCI?"

"Either lost or consumed. I don't know."

"I can find out," she said.

I raised my eyebrows.

"Why do you think Joe approached me?"

"Is that his name?"

"Yeah. I don't know if it's real or his last name. I'd say he's around fifty-five years old. Good-looking guy, but he's been around. His eyes give me chills."

"What part of the CIA?"

"He didn't say."

"How do you know if you can trust him?"

"I can't."

"How do you know you aren't being set up?"

"I don't, but from what I can drag up, he's for real. I think we'd be better off not digging too deep into his past."

"This isn't a small deal. This involves teams of people. How do you expect to make this happen? Or me, for that matter?"

"He's got the teams. He needs the finesse that I provide to ensure there is a perceived cover-up. I'm acting more as a consultant for him. I agreed to help provided I am not made known to any of his colleagues. He agreed."

"And you believe him?"

"He may have dead eyes, but he looks like a guy who keeps his word."

I looked at her from across the breakfast table. Sex with her was still mind-blowing, and I still distrusted her, but I found her certainty contagious. I was also looking for something more to do than sit around. I was bored. This was the perfect tonic.

"So, our job is to locate drug money and funnel it towards the East German economy in the hope that it bankrupts itself while orchestrating a scandal that may take down the presidency, and promote war on our near borders."

"I'm not sure why you keep repeating yourself. You're smarter than this, George."

"Pass the coffee. We need to be clever when it comes to the East Germans."

She pursed her lips. Her cheeks were still flush. The sunlight that came through the windows gleamed off the white in her outfit. She was waiting for the wheels to stop turning in my head, for me to catch up to her.

The coffee passed my lips and I pushed in some toast for good measure. I stared at the ceiling, mind clicking and dismissing various scenarios.

"Bankruptcy won't mean anything unless the entity they are defaulting against can prevent them from getting any further credit." I said it slowly as the thoughts began to form in my head. "This means only a loan from the IMF or similar agency will have the affect we are after."

Sylvia was silent.

"We need to recommend that they get spies inside East Germany to promote the genius of microchip production. That seems to be their Achilles' heel. Assuming it will be a disaster, we get East Germany to approach the International Monetary Fund to broker a loan of hard currency to allow it to build and sell products to the outside world and solve its crisis."

I liked where my mind was going. Sylvia remained silent.

"As long as the rest of the world thinks that the country is working to dig itself out, it will assume that any collapse is the result of an incompetent central government. The big question is whether Moscow rescues it."

"We can't influence that," Sylvia said. "We can only create points of crisis. It's like spinning the wheel. We won't know if we win or lose until it stops."

"But we are placing big bets. If we win, we create a massive crack in the empire."

"Without a shot being fired," she added.

"I doubt that. Revolutions always spill blood." I poured more coffee and drank it. "Many a slip between lip and cup," I mumbled.

"Huh?"

"A lot of things can go wrong with this plan."

"So you're in?" She was leaning forward. She seemed to know me better than I knew myself.

"I wouldn't miss this for the world," I said.

Chapter Twelve

Power

"Some of our greatest patriots will never be known by the public. It is a burden some of us bear."

I looked around to see President-elect Bush. His security guards were two steps away but he wanted to talk to me. I think he wanted to give me advice or console me that I did the right thing. Even now, three years after Sylvia pitched the plan, I wasn't sure it was a good idea. Too late now, though.

"Sir," I said. I stood instinctively. I noticed his bodyguards make a half step towards me at the sudden movement.

"Please, sit down. May I join you?"

I wasn't going to say no. We were at the Rockefeller Center at a fundraiser or congratulatory ball or something. I could never keep track. In the years since I parted company from the bank and all its seedy clients, I had hired two personal assistants. They told me where

I needed to be and I rarely cared about the labels. I knew it all amounted to the same thing—a plea for money, usually by politicians or judges looking to be re-elected, often by bleeding hearts looking to alter the perceived injustices of the world. There were impassioned pleas, vigorous applause, and faces flush from alcohol and power. It was a day out for the rich and the price of admission was a donation. Today was no different, except that I was talking to the future president of the United States.

"I will be inviting you to the Oval Office at some point during my administration. I want you to know that. But in addition, I wanted to say thank you on behalf of a grateful nation. Your sacrifice, dedication, and hard work will go unrecognized in history, but its impact has been registered by those who count."

I looked at his intensity. He sat close, ensuring no one could hear him. I think he even positioned himself so that people couldn't read his lips. He was tall and athletic, and more powerful in person than I would have guessed. The media presented him as the invisible man or the wimp. I knew he was former CIA and that he was rich. More than that, I didn't know. Right now, he was shaking my hand.

"Thank you, sir. I was just doing my duty."

"We need more men like you in this country, George. People have become seduced by the dollar and the sense of easy money. You have proved to me that you can take the man out of service but you can't take the service out of the man. You're a good soldier."

I was beginning to feel awkward at the praise. I said nothing and nodded.

"I want to introduce you to someone whom I think will help you in your journey."

"Journey?"

"In making the world a better place."

"Sir, I'm just an ordinary guy."

"With talent. Don't sell yourself short. Not just anyone could have done what you did. I know there's been a lot of noise but we were ready for it." He became quiet and I saw his eyes lift up and to the right, as though he was remembering something. "The president survived the storm, and the foundation has been laid for some historic changes in the world."

"Sir, I hope I've done my part, but I haven't seen any impact on things."

"You will." He got up and put his hand on my shoulder. "And have a good rest of the evening."

I stood up and shook his hand. I almost saluted him. He had a firm grip and steely eye. He was different from what I expected. I waited for him to disappear behind his moving wall of secret agents. I sat down and finished my drink.

"What was that all about?" said a more familiar and welcome voice. I felt her hand across my shoulders and then down my back. Her perfume increased my temperature.

"That was the most bizarre encounter I have ever had, and that's saying a lot."

"What did he say?" Sylvia sat next to me and put her hand on my leg. I put my hand on hers.

"I think he was saying that we did a good job, but he didn't seem to know about you."

Her lips pursed as she tried to restrain a smile. "Sorry about that. I needed them to know who was behind everything. I couldn't let them know about me if I wanted to stay anonymous." Sylvia glanced at the people who began to crowd their space ever since the secret service agents and President-elect Bush left. I wasn't worried about being overheard. No-one knew who either of us were. Just to be safe, I moved in closer to Sylvia.

"What about Joe?"

"He knows. He's my handler, but he's not stupid enough to give up his assets. I hope you don't mind. It's only for the glory. I wouldn't have said anything if it failed."

"If it failed, we'd both be fish food."

Sylvia ordered a champagne and I nodded for another scotch.

"You're so dramatic."

"We just about took down Reagan."

"He couldn't be taken down. He's indestructible."

"Hmm." *No one is indestructible*, I thought.

"We accomplished our goal."

"Russia is as strong as ever," I said.

"Not from what I hear."

"Propaganda. It doesn't rely on us. It's self-sufficient."

"But GDR isn't."

"East Germany may fall, but it doesn't mean Russia will. That's fantasy thinking."

"What's got into you?" she said. She looked concerned.

"We spent nearly three years on this. I almost got killed, twice. What do we get for it? A pat on the back by the president-elect, no public credit, and the reassurance that we are patriots."

"You. I'm invisible, remember?"

"Yeah. I keep reminding myself that you're smarter than me."

She liked that and leaned in to kiss me briefly.

"Bush was head of the CIA. He knew exactly what was happening," she said.

"He was CIA. He was vice-president when we were sucked into this."

"Once CIA, always CIA." She smiled at me over her glass.

"You're saying he greenlit this project?"

"Who else?"

"Reagan?"

"He didn't know about it."

"How do you know?"

"I've heard things about him."

"You know that hacking is going to get you in trouble."

"It'll keep me safe. I'm going all J. Edgar Hoover on them. I've got files developing that'll make your head spin."

"Careful, Sylvia. These guys aren't the boy scouts."

"You're telling me. I wouldn't be surprised if Bush doesn't invade a few countries to settle come outstanding debts."

I raised my eyebrows.

"Noriega? Drug smuggling? Laundering money? Reagan put him in charge of stopping drugs from entering the country. On his watch, by some accounts, the Columbians made almost fifty billion dollars selling drugs. Where do you think they stash it? Panama. If I were a betting girl, I'd clear out my accounts from Panama. They're going to hit him and take his money."

"It's not his money," I said.

"But if it's tied to drugs, they'll take it and worry about who it belongs to later. Of all people, you should know that everything leads back to money."

I opened my mouth, then closed it. She had a point.

Sylvia was wearing a dress that covered every inch of her body, from her wrists to her ankles. It sat on her in ways that made her sexier than if she was naked. Her curves and movements were accentuated. I caught flashes of light in the fabric. I took her hand and lifted it to my lips.

"Care to dance?"

"I thought you'd never ask. Perhaps you thought all this talk was foreplay?" She stood and allowed me to lead her.

"It was," I said over my shoulder.

∞

I was in a funny place. I had lots of money and I lived with a beautiful woman. Sylvia had moved back in shortly after I returned to New York. I had tasted international intrigue and subterfuge—both in service to my country and in direct opposition to it. I had rolled the dice and won. I stepped over the line of legality and back before anyone caught me. Part of me was disappointed that it was even possible.

To top it all off, I was approaching fifty years old. My stomach was developing a slight paunch. My hair was both thinning and greying. I noticed that I was becoming invisible to younger women—until they realized how rich I was. But I wasn't interested in those. I knew Sylvia would tire of me some day. I didn't understand why she was still around. She was approaching thirty and would want children at some point. I didn't. That would end that.

The future president of the United States patted me on the back. I was known in secret circles unreported to the general public. I was on the radar. Yet none of it excited me. There was no amount of money that would make me feel richer. I had more money than I could ever spend during my lifetime. There was no woman who could be smarter, funnier, or sexier than Sylvia. I was in good health and had no overtly hostile enemies.

But it wasn't enough.

Public office didn't appeal to me. I considered any publicity dangerous and unnecessary. I had learned long ago that the real power existed in the shadows. No president, however popular, was his own man. No general followed himself. No one I knew had both power and true freedom. We all make bargains, compromises, and choices. I was lucky enough in mine, but getting what I wanted didn't give me what I needed.

I wanted the girl at the top of the tower to tell me she loved me. I wanted it then. Now was too late. I didn't know how to reconcile it.

I got up. I didn't want to wake Sylvia. I decided to go for a walk. The sun was just rising and the city, while it never truly slept, was waking up. I would find a bakery and tear open some fresh bread and share it with the birds in Central Park. I would have got a dog if I lived a more stationary life. I loved the simplicity and honesty of animals.

The air held moisture as nature fought itself, brushing off the night air and embracing the day. I found a small bakery and then an empty bench. It was covered with dew. I let my overcoat absorb it. It wouldn't reach my skin. The coffee was good and I watched the dawn joggers and dog walkers. I tried to understand the motivation that caused them to run in circles—exercise for its own sake and nothing to show for their efforts but a sweaty bundle of clothes and muscles that would cramp if they didn't do it again tomorrow.

I was rich, so why wasn't I happy?

Chapter Thirteen

Dominoes

"Now do you think it was all a waste of time?"

"I never said it was a waste of time. I didn't believe anything we did could cause this."

"A small crack can break a dam," Sylvia said.

"Yeah, but this?"

"I've packed my hammer and chisel."

"I'm sure they're selling them by the truckloads over there."

The plane took off and I felt Sylvia's hand in mine. She was more excited than I was. When she first heard that the wall was coming done, she called me and booked the tickets. We wanted to dance with the rest of the Berliners—with the added knowledge that we had more than a little part in making it happen.

The wall will go down in history as opening on the ninth day of November, 1989. We arrived on the tenth. We checked into the Waldorf Astoria, perhaps because we didn't know any better. It was more modern than we expected, but we had no intention of spending much time sleeping.

"Where do you want to go?"

"Where else? The Brandenburg Gate." I decided one chisel between us was enough and we went to get ourselves a souvenir.

I was surprised to see firemen and police either erecting or deconstructing a structure at the place in the wall we wanted to go. I looked to my left and saw a sea of people with chisels taking chunks of the wall, and we joined them. It was covered with graffiti.

"Did I mention that the wall is full of asbestos?" I was a little concerned, but didn't figure our brief encounter would mean our demise.

"Yeah, yeah. Did I mention that smoking kills?" Sylvia didn't miss a beat. She was working on a piece the size of a dinner plate. Our initial attempts failed. The concrete was exceptionally hard. The finished surface was smoother and had a white base under the graffiti. The difficulty was in being able to chisel in deep enough to to take a solid piece of concrete, complete with its spray-painted finish.

"Maybe we should hire some of these locals to do it," I said. I looked over and saw some of the youngsters walking away with the exact-sized pieces we were trying to extract.

"This is a piece of cake. I just need time. I can't believe how impatient you are." She never looked at me and concentrated on her task like a surgeon.

There was an energy in the air I had never experienced before. I tried to see if I could distinguish the East Germans from their western counterparts. I gave up when I realized that the entire world was represented around me. The mood was a mixture of hope and fear—hope that nearly three decades of forced separation was over, and fear that it would be snatched away without explanation. Everyone watched the East German guards nervously. From where I stood, they weren't visible. There was the wall I faced, a dog run, a second wall, and then the guards. I saw them on the news, though, and at the other side of Checkpoint Charlie. They stood with guns to their sides, watching in as much disbelief as us.

"The power of a simple command," I said as much to myself as Sylvia.

"Huh?" She wasn't going to be distracted.

"One Russian, Khrushchev, decides to make an example of Berlin. One American, Kennedy, decides to as well. Two global powers go nose-to-nose with the world in the balance, and this wall symbolizes it all."

"Yep." All I could hear was the staccato of her chisel and those around me.

"And yesterday, Gorbachev must have given the order not to do anything. It was the same as allowing the wall to fall."

"Hmm. Stop talking and put your hand here. I think I've got it." She hit her chisel with precision and I felt the piece release. It wasn't as big as we had hoped, but it was a great souvenir.

"Wonderful." I kissed her and tasted the beginning of a salty residue. She must have been working hard.

"That was satisfying. Shall we take in the sights?"

"I thought this was the only sight in town," I said.

"It's not going anywhere for a few days, maybe years. Let's stay for a while."

I had no problem with that and we began walking back to our hotel. There were too many people and we couldn't have found a taxi if we wanted to.

"This must be the biggest news around the world. It looks like every television station is here," I said.

"The news is like looking through a rear view mirror. They never report accurately enough to allow you to see what's coming."

"How can they? The real reason the wall fell will be redacted for decades. Historians may never figure it all out. It makes me wonder about the versions of history that I thought I understood. There is so much more that we will never know."

"Still think that hacking is a waste of time?" she said. "How else will we ever find out the truth?"

Her hair was pulled back and we both wore light jackets. Winter hadn't yet struck. Her prize was stuck under her arm. I carried the hammer and chisel. I saw a red-haired guy with a Canadian flag sewn onto his backpack walking towards the wall. He didn't have a chisel so I gave him ours. It was a perfect day.

The hotel was full of excited faces and they all turned to see what Sylvia held in her hands. They nodded in silent appreciation and we nodded back. Our ears and bodies took a moment to acclimatize to the silence of the hotel. Muzac played unobtrusively in the background and more noticeably in the elevator. A man slipped into it with us at the last moment, causing the doors to open and wait again before closing.

I saw Sylvia's face change and I was going to ask her what happened when her eyes told me to stay silent. She was staring at the man. He stood with his back to the wall looking ahead, but seeing both of us through the reflection. He looked to be perhaps sixty years old. He had a few days' stubble on his face, all grey. His jacket was grey tweed and looked tailored. If it wasn't for Sylvia's reaction, I wouldn't have taken a second look at him.

"This your floor?" he said when the door opened. He stood aside and let us out. He nodded to Sylvia as the doors closed.

"Do you know that guy?"

She was shaken. She went to our room, put the concrete on the table, and pulled out four little bottles from the minibar and began sucking them back.

"Whoa. Slow down, sweetheart. What's the matter?"

"That's him."

"Who? It looks like you saw a ghost."

"Joe."

My head moved back six inches and I stood up straight. Every part of my body strained against its senses.

"What's he doing here?"

"Checking up on us? Congratulating us?" She looked nervous. She never looked nervous, and it made me uneasy.

"Killing us?" I couldn't help myself. We had done our job. We were no longer essential.

"Then why show himself to us?" she said.

"I don't know. I have a feeling we're going to find out soon enough."

"Then I'm going to go out in style." She picked up the phone next to the bed. "Hello? Yes, I would like to speak to the spa. It is? Great. Do you have a slot today? Twenty minutes. I'll be there. Yes, Öst. Great. See you soon." I don't know why she didn't speak in German. It was one of the languages she was fluent in. I think she liked being thought of as a stupid American tourist. It allowed her to hear what they really thought of her when they least anticipated it. She never showed all her cards.

"Is that wise?"

"Why not? If he's here to kill us, I want to be relaxed. I have a feeling he wants to talk."

"Why didn't he talk in the elevator?"

"I don't know. Paranoid? Cameras? He may not want any record of us interacting."

I thought for a moment and picked up the phone. They had a second slot available. I liked the idea of being pampered before I died. It was a lot better than the alternative.

∞

"Foot massage?"

"Sure. We're booked in the room with two massage tables. We can see each other and talk if we want, but it won't be ready for another half hour. We can take in a foot massage."

"One of my favorite massages was in Shanghai. It was forty minutes long on the foot and calf. Most of us fell asleep. It was like magic. I hope I'm not ruined."

"Snob," she said with a smile.

Our foot stations had a curtain drawn between us. I pulled it back so I could see Sylvia. If these were our last moments alive, I wanted to make the most of them.

The foot massage was amazing, and the full body massage took away all our worries. Ninety minutes of warm medicated oils. Neither of us spoke, but turned our heads so that we could see each other if we wanted to. We returned to the pool and relaxed on the chaise lounges. Our robes were extra fluffy and I was content.

"Is this chair taken?" The voice was warm and inviting. I opened my eyes and saw Joe. All benefits of the massages were lost in an instant.

"Hello, Joe," I said. Sylvia was sitting up by now.

"So you know who I am," he said. He sat on the edge of my chair, looking at the two of us.

"I don't think anyone knows who you are," Sylvia said.

He seemed to appreciate that and I noticed a small smile.

"I'm not here to kill you, if that's what you're thinking."

"I gathered as much," I said. "We're not dead." *Yet*, I thought.

"I would like to talk. There's something you need to know. Some people I'm looking for."

"Taking down East Germany wasn't enough for you?" I said. There weren't many people in the pool or chairs. Even if there were, they wouldn't take notice.

Sylvia was right; his eyes were dead. I felt a chill as he looked at me. "It wasn't the objective. I wanted to flush out some people. We didn't succeed because the damn plan worked."

I was confused.

"You mean all of this was some bullshit tail-chasing exercise?" Sylvia said.

"No, the premise of our actions was real. The VP signed off, and all of the players agreed. Why do you think Reagan included that phrase in his speech?"

"Mr. Gorbachev, tear down this wall?" I parroted. My Reagan impression wasn't that good, but it got a little grin from Joe.

"Exactly. We applied pressure from all angles, including financial. I had assumed another group would have surfaced during the exercise."

"What kind of group?"

"The group that orchestrates wars, manipulates currencies, and controls governments."

"Oh, that group," I said sarcastically. "Joe, we're done with the bullshit. We're not going to swallow some story of a shadowy group that rules the world. It is a weak-minded story perpetrated by people who want to blame others for their failures."

"I always suspected you may have been lying to us, Joe," Sylvia said. "Why tell us this now? Why not let us feel like we were part of something important?" Her eyes were red but not from tears.

"I know I sound crazy," he said. "If I didn't know what I know, I would be saying the same thing as you. This is personal for me. The last mission was sanctioned, but the next one isn't."

"Next one?"

"You proved yourselves as good as any government organization with a hundred times the resources. I have always preferred working in small groups. I believe we can be more effective, more disruptive against the enemy."

"Enemy?" I didn't like him sitting on my chaise lounge. He was the same size as me and I felt cramped.

"Anyone who interferes with your will is your enemy. You decide if you do something about it or not."

"Don't spoil this by talking crazy talk. What do you want from us?" Sylvia was losing her sense of humor.

"My best years are behind me, but I've got one last kick at this can. Let me explain it this way. There are a handful of people who meet in secret and co-ordinate their actions to affect world events. I agree that no one can control the world, but soft power is an effective tool. When it controls people with hard power—armies and weapons—that becomes a force multiplier. All of this is made possible by a world that is run on credit. They control the credit. Their goal has been to homogenize global credit solely to ensure that they are the gatekeepers. They plan and act in decades, not days. The mission to act as catalysts in the implosion of East Germany using foreign debt is exactly the type of trick they excel at."

I was looking at him as though he was Jon Roberts on cocaine.

"How long have you been watching us?" I asked.

"Only since I met Sylvia. More serendipity than anything else." He paused before adding, "Once I began to monitor you, I knew I could trust you. I put two and two together and figured that it was you who ran those operations in Laos."

I looked at Sylvia. She shrugged. I didn't want to start that conversation. There were only a handful of people who knew what I did, and I had no intention of volunteering information.

"What do you want to do with this group?"

"They call themselves the Order. I think the full name is Order of Prime, don't ask me why. The problem is that I can't figure out who is in the group. The last member I knew of had an accident and died."

I couldn't read his expression. I remained silent.

"But if I could find them, I'd kill them all."

Chapter Fourteen

Hitting Bottom

I thought about my parents. They lived in obscurity on a farm in the middle of nowhere. They had enough. Even with less, they would still have enough. They never talked about money, even when it was tight. If I did overhear anything, it was unavoidable, such as when they were served with legal papers or when they almost lost the farm. Those events still feel like yesterday for me; for them, it is ancient history. I try to protect myself by gathering more money; they live their lives with what they have. I don't know why I don't cope the same way as they do. I realized I would never become rich enough to be safe. Or happy.

Then Sylvia walked in the room wearing her bra and underwear, and she was like a light to my darkness. I felt a glow grow inside me. I realized that this must be what my parents felt together. I began to have hope.

"He's crazy, you know," she said as she pulled on some jeans. I liked that she ironed her jeans.

"He's a survivor," I said. "Definitely a vet. Probably an assassin. Most likely CIA, but black ops. Without a doubt, crazy."

"But is he dangerous?"

"Only to his enemies."

"You mean, anyone who interferes with his will?"

"I didn't like that part either," I said. "What, do we kill someone for bumping into us while we're crossing the street?"

"Whatever the case, he's intense. I don't think we have a choice." She was pinning up her hair and I admired her lithe arms.

"In other words, our will is bent to his?"

"Yep." She leaned over and kissed me before she put on her lipstick.

"There may be nothing we can do," I said.

"Then there's nothing to worry about." She continued dressing. I found it odd how calm she was.

"We're supposed to wait until he sees an opportunity?"

"I'll be looking as well."

"What am I supposed to do?"

"Look handsome, read, write, and relax."

A switch had changed in her wiring. She had gone into survival mode and it didn't allow for anger, fear, or anxiety. I couldn't believe this was the same woman who was so passionate. I envied her focus and control.

My skills weren't irrelevant for this new task, yet I was on standby. Somewhere deep in my mind, a voice spoke to the incongruences. I knew it was a red flag. I decided to ignore it. It was the power I gave women I loved. I wanted happiness more than I wanted to be right.

"You're going to go with Joe by yourself and hunt down those monsters?" I had dismissed the suggestion out of hand when he raised it. She was equivocal. I think she liked the challenge and admired his unyielding character.

She nodded solemnly.

It was the worst of all scenarios for me. I was like a married man living a retired life with his wife running off with another man. I didn't know if she was having an affair, the time of her life, or both. I was expected to wait while they pursued some fantasy. What was I supposed to do while I waited? Play golf? I hated golf. I didn't want to become one of those guys who rotted away his days waiting to die. That wasn't living; it was barely existing.

She kissed me again, this time slowly as if to remind me that she loved me. I believed her. When she left, the click of the door closing rang in my ears.

∞

I waited for a day before I became worried. Not a call, message, or letter. After two days, I thought I should call the police. Then I remembered who I was dealing with. After a week, I decided to return to New York and wait for her there. She would eventually come back. She always did.

The flight was fitful. I refused to take sleeping pills and I had no taste for alcohol. I couldn't find anything to read that interested me. The newspapers blackened my fingers before I gave up trying. There was a brief layover in Frankfurt, uneventful, and I was soon watching the cabin lights dim as we flew over the Atlantic. I couldn't sleep and I had seen the movie before.

My body ached for the comforts of my own bed, the familiar smells of my apartment, and the unlimited options available to me in New York. I was beginning to understand that she left me. I shouldn't be surprised; it was always just a matter of time. I hurt, but not as much as I did over Barbie. I don't think I could handle that type of pain again.

The taxi ride was almost as exhausting as the flight. I developed an anxiety over thoughts of dating new women. I was happy with Sylvia. Suddenly I understood why I wasn't kicking at the walls. I was happy, but not in love, with Sylvia. I began to smile at this revelation and wanted the journey to end. The traffic was stationary and more than once, I thought of walking. The driver must have been able to see my inner struggles and he reassured me each time that things were fine and it would be easier to be driven than to walk.

I slumped further into my seat, resigning myself to traffic, loneliness, and fate.

I gave him a big tip, handed my bags to the porter, and walked to the elevator. I didn't wait for my bags. He could catch the next one. He would also bring up any parcels or recorded post that had been received in my absence. I would deal with it tomorrow.

The sound of the key in my security door was like music. Its weight reassured me that everything would be okay. I left the door open a crack and walked inside. I wanted to draw the curtains back to take in my view.

I turned to get a drink when I sensed another person in the room. I saw her on my sofa, holding a gun.

"George?"

"Yes?"

I forced my eyes to focus. "Jasmine?"

"I'm sorry it has to end this way." She raised the gun and I looked down the barrel. For some reason, I began to laugh.

"What's so funny?" she said. She kept the gun aimed at me.

"Now that I'm dead, I'm no longer afraid. My entire life, every second of every day was about my future, my plans. It's all bullshit, isn't it?"

"Sometimes."

"And I bet when this moment comes, everyone becomes focused."

"Not everyone. Most blubber or promise me money or try forgiveness."

"But there's nothing to forgive, is there?"

She shook her head.

"No amount that would make you or them reconsider?"

She shook her head.

"A million?"

I felt a pain like nothing I had felt before tear through my right shoulder. My arm went limp.

"Ten?"

I could barely stand when the next bullet slammed through my left shoulder. My arms were useless and I fell backwards into the glass window. It held my weight and I slid down.

"Hundred?"

She paused, then walked next to me. She put the barrel on my forehead. I felt the warmed metal move, never leaving my skin. It traced my nose, lips, chin, and chest. She didn't say a word.

It drifted to my crotch. She paused, then continued down my leg. At my knee, she used the barrel to find the soft spot she was looking for. She angled the barrel as though she was going to shoot through the side of my knee, under the kneecap. I opened my mouth to say something when she pulled the trigger. The pain was too much for me and I may have passed out.

"You have thirty minutes. I hope your banker knows your voice."

At least I was alive.

"If he hears my pain, he won't transfer."

"Not my problem."

The pain was blinding. "I'm going to bleed out before you'll get your money."

Jasmine looked me over before she reached for the phone. "Emergency? There's been a burglary. No, I don't want to get involved. Yes. Please get here as soon as possible. Multiple gunshot wounds. Yes. Gunshots." She gave the address and put the phone down.

"You've bought yourself a week. Make the arrangements. I'll get you the bank details. Pray you don't ever see me again."

I watched her and wondered what was broken in her to cause such cruelty. I've only been good to her. She must have been promoted after she took the CIA drug money. Now she was taking my Colombian drug money. But why was she there to kill me?

I didn't figure it out before everything went black.

∞

When I woke up, I saw my father sitting in the hospital chair next to me. It wasn't long before my mother arrived, then the tears, and then the love rained down on me. They nourished me with unadulterated parental love. I felt like I was the most precious thing in the world. When I smiled, their faces lit up.

I made arrangements for the hundred million to be paid and I waited to see Sylvia or Joe. Neither came. When I was discharged, I returned to where I knew I was always welcome.

Our farm was a mile out of town and a good drive from Chicago. They had a new dog and a couple of cats had adopted them. They didn't ask any questions. Whatever happened was irrelevant. I felt safe and loved.

I wasn't broke, but I would never be rich again. I still had over a hundred million safely stashed away. I would need to find a way to live with the knowledge that I will never be the biggest or the richest. I would only be kind of rich.

A sense of loss washed over me. I had nothing. Yes, I had some money, but Sylvia's betrayal left a hole as large as Barbie's. I still couldn't fathom Jasmine's behavior or motive. Was I such a bad guy? Was I so unlovable?

∞

Life on a working farm had a rhythm I had forgotten. My parents were now too old to milk cows or till the fields. They still woke early and oversaw the daily upkeep of equipment and stock. My father could never just sit after his morning coffee. He wanted to put his hands on the animals and make sure the men were doing what they were supposed to.

I tagged along, all the while re-living memories. I never understood what the CIA saw in me to give away so much power and authority. I didn't understand why Jon Roberts decided that I was the best person to launder the Medellin cartel's money.

"Watch out, son."

I returned to the present to see my father's face. I followed his eyes too late. I was already in it.

"Don't worry, George. It's good luck to step in cow shit."

"Argh," I said. "I guess I need to start watching where I'm going."

My father put his hand on my shoulder. "They're not chasing you here. Relax. Everything will be all right."

I wanted to cry. I wished I had his absolute belief. "I don't think anything will be okay ever again," I said.

Dad faced me and put both hands on my shoulders. "Life is what you make it. That's all I've learned. Being happy or sad? Barring some medical condition, it is a choice."

"Finding a girlfriend who doesn't betray or shoot you?"

"Unlucky." Dad left the word hanging and smiled. I smiled back. He started laughing, and I couldn't help myself. He had a point.

We continued our rounds and returned to the house. Mom had fresh coffee ready and we all relaxed into the kitchen chairs as we went through the various things that needed to be done. It was all important but nothing was life or death. Or perhaps that's because Dad never let it feel that way.

"I need to go to Chicago for some parts. Want to join me?"

I had nothing else to do. "Sure."

"Coming, hon?"

"I think I'll stay home and relax. You two enjoy yourselves."

There was always conversation on the farm, but it flowed over me like soft clouds. There was no urgency or even the need to listen. Just being there informed me what needed to be done. My body language was enough. A nod, shrug, or thumbs up was all the workers needed. It was so different from the drug-fueled orgies of Miami or war crimes of Laos and Vietnam.

I felt the jolt as if my body slapped me awake. Being home, I could finally see the tensions I lived with in my pursuit of money. I wasn't being true to myself.

Who am I? A farm boy with big ambitions. A kid who wanted love, then money, and failed at both. A man who sacrificed his soul to gain the world, only for it to turn to ashes.

I could still feel the barrel of the gun against my head. I wished Jasmine had pulled the trigger. The truck rumbled over the dirt roads and I couldn't wait to hit the interstate. Dad let me drive and the monotony was my meditation.

"You know they wanted to kill me," I said.

Dad was silent. I saw him nodding.

"I haven't been a very good person, Dad."

"You did what you thought you needed to do."

"No, I did whatever it took to make big money."

"Isn't that the way of the world?"

"Not your world."

"Your mom and I are lucky."

"Why can't I find a girl like her?"

"Were you looking?" He looked at me.

It was a good point. I wasn't. Each girl found me. Jasmine, as part of her mission. Sylvia, because that was her nature.

"I thought it would just happen."

"Nothing just happens, son. We need to want it to happen, and we need to grab hold of it when it does."

"I did that. I chased money and accumulated a lot of it. But I don't feel rich."

"Money is only part of being rich," he said. "You need to be who you are. You can act and fool others. But you can't fool yourself forever."

I didn't agree but I was in no position to talk. Perhaps I was sabotaging myself without even knowing it.

PART TWO

The Others

Chapter Fifteen

G29

"A bit dramatic, don't you think?"

"I'm sorry, sir."

"All we needed from the poor sap was the money. I think he still has a lot more."

"I let my emotions get in the way. It won't happen again."

"Jasmine, I was always concerned about this mission."

"The first one was easier," she said. "I guess I became attached to him. When I saw him again, I felt jealous. It doesn't make any sense."

"You did a fine job. No one is complaining."

"General?"

"Yes?"

"I think there may be others."

"Of course there are others. He couldn't have done this by himself."

"A woman."

"Ah. Is this the green-eyed monster raising its head again?"

"No, I think she's been recruited by someone else."

"One of ours?"

"I don't know. Possibly, but he was rambling on about something called the Order."

"Never heard of it."

"I didn't hear it directly. An agent was stationed in Berlin. She heard it, but nothing she says makes sense."

"No recordings?"

"The woman is paranoid. She sweeps for bugs like a mad woman."

"Apparently with some reason."

"How could she know?"

"Just cautious. We could all learn from her."

"What do you want me to do about her?"

"Nothing. She's a technician."

"What about the man?"

"Get me a name."

"I can do one better." Jasmine looked down as she put her hand into her briefcase. She found what she needed and pulled it out. "Here's his photo. We managed to get a partial hit on him. He served in Korea in communications under the name Max Harding. There's been no record on him in the army or any of the services since. He just disappeared."

"Yet, here he is. Have you searched CIA records?"

"Affirmative. Nothing."

"Maybe he's her long lost uncle. I don't think he's anyone to worry about, for now. Focus on the girl."

"Yes, sir. Anything else, General?"

"No. You've done well."

"Thank you, sir." Jasmine saluted and left General Calhoun's office.

As the door closed, Calhoun sat heavily into his chair. His office was sparse and efficient. There was the hidden liquor cabinet, the scores of pictures with him shaking presidents' hands, and his old service photos. His eye returned to the one photo that continued to haunt him. In it, he and his wife were smiling with their son. It had been a good day.

The buzzer on his desk jarred him back to the present.

"Yes?"

"Your next appointment is ready to see you, sir."

"Not here."

"No, sir. Your driver is waiting for you."

"I'll be right there."

Calhoun went to the drinks cabinet and poured himself a soda. As he drank, his eyes fixed on the colored bottles. Most officers stocked the cheapest whiskey, but he kept a dozen different single malts as well as the usual gins and vodkas. There was an unopened bottle of rum in the back that no one had yet requested.

As he walked out, he grabbed his hat and overcoat and slung it over his arm. He was at the top of the pyramid and every soldier scrambled when he entered a room. He used to like it, but he now avoided them when he could.

The door to the Suburban was open and he slid into the back seat. It closed without him touching it and he felt the vehicle begin to move. The two soldiers in the front were silent, one driving and one for show.

It wasn't a long drive, but they needed to get off base. That took almost ten minutes, and it was a further half hour to the meeting spot. It had been a long time since he had met anyone there.

"This is fine, Captain."

"Sir."

The captain pulled the government-issue four-wheel drive next to the edge of the hangar. He left the engine running as he opened his door and then the general's.

"Stick around. I don't know how long I'll be."

"Yes, sir."

The two saluted and Calhoun walked towards the steel door. It was unlocked. The lights were on inside.

"Hello?" His voice sounded empty. There was no plane in the hangar. It was meant for a small craft, probably a private Lear or large prop. It was clean with the smell of cold oil and metal. At least it was above freezing inside.

"Calhoun, you sonofabitch! How's it going?"

He smiled despite himself. "Max. It's been a long time."

Joe came out of the shadows into the middle of the building. They shook hands, then Calhoun pulled him into a short bear-hug.

"Korea, at least."

"I think I saw some shadows of your handiwork," Calhoun said.

"Then I must be getting rusty."

The general put his arm around his friend. "We're all getting older."

"Speak for yourself," Joe said.

"How's the girl?"

"Like I said, speak for yourself."

The two men laughed. They made their way to the internal office where the heat would allow them to speak more comfortably.

"I've got a small problem," the general said.

"Only one?" Joe hadn't shaved in a few days and the stubble formed a white patina across his face. His clothes were un-ironed, as though he were a bachelor. Nothing spoke to his impeccable military past.

"The GDR operation. I know it was you."

"And?"

"These types of operations are bigger than you. This is why we have infrastructure."

"It's too big. Too many leaks. The mission would have been compromised. Besides, I didn't do anything spectacular."

"You helped take down a country, Max. From the looks of things, it may be the first domino of many."

Joe grinned. "My parting contribution."

"Your lucky contribution."

"I'd rather be lucky than smart."

"You're both and you know it, which is why I'm here."

Joe was silent.

"I've been bleeding your contact."

"That was you?"

It was Calhoun's turn to grin. "That sonofabitch stole from the US government. I just took what was rightly ours."

"And returned it to the US government?"

"I returned it to a department that can make better use of it."

"Our old unit?"

"Our current unit. You know how it is."

"We are becoming more like chameleons every day. I'm concerned at how large G29 is becoming. Soon, it'll become overrun by pencil pushers rather than people who get things done."

"Like you," Calhoun said.

"Exactly. And you know that first hand."

Calhoun was silent.

"So that's why Sylvia found out," Joe said. "She was right. I was doubtful."

"She knows?"

"She seems to get into everything. You need to figure out how to work those damn computers. It'll be the Achilles' heel of the organization."

"Hmm. And she won't be turned?" The general was beginning to like her.

Joe tensed. "No. That was my deal with her. I'd let her stay and operate in anonymity provided she gives me the information I need."

"Isn't that the same as working for us?"

"She isn't doing it for any reason other than that she loves breaking into things. She's like an idiot savant."

"I saw her picture. She's no Rain Man."

Joe laughed. "That, she isn't."

"I guess you're not going to tell me the rest of her story?"

"You guessed right." Joe couldn't keep the mirth from his face.

"And you're going by a different name. Joe, is it?"

"Yeah. Easier this way."

The general paused. "And you need our help. Why now?"

"It's personal. I just need access to resources."

"Officially or…"

"Just let Sylvia access everything. She'll do the rest. Passwords, new structures, that sort of thing. I've been trying to get out of this damn place but there's no way. I may as well embrace it and use it for my ends."

"That could be treason, Max. We would both hang for it."

"Yes, we might. But at least we'll hang for serving our country."

Calhoun took a deep breath and exhaled slowly. "I need a cigarette. I'm getting too old for this shit."

"Are you planning to quote movies or make decisions?"

"When did you become such an insolent sonofabitch?"

"The day I realized there weren't enough days in my life to kill all the bastards."

They looked at each other and Calhoun broke first.

"I miss you, man. You're one crazy motherfucker."

"Crazy motherfucker, sir."

"Alright. What exactly do you want from me?"

Chapter Sixteen

The Order

"These are interesting times, aren't they?"

"Most certainty, Lady Teignmouth."

"Do we have any news from the rest of the group?"

"Not yet. Things are moving quickly and, well, we don't."

"Yes, quite rightly too. Nothing worse than being reactionary."

The chandeliers threw off a yellow glow in the dark paneled room. Paintings of ancestors glared from the walls. The table was set for three. The other eight would join them another day. Lady Teignmouth, haughty for being made to wait, watched the door and dismissed her maid. Her countenance lifted as soon as she saw who came through it.

"Good morning, Lady Teignmouth."

"Wonderful to see you again, Mr. Rock. Please have a seat."

"Mr. Roth should only be a moment. Do accept our apologies for making you wait."

"Not at all," she said, waving her hand. "I understand. Tea?"

"I would love one. I imagine Mr. Roth will have one too."

"Splendid." She pushed a small button on the floor with her foot and her maid appeared, took instructions, and left.

Mr. Rock was American. Mr. Roth and Lady Teignmouth were English. The three formed the core of the Order of Prime. They understood, without articulating, that their will was followed by the whole.

"Mr. Roth, how do you see events?" He arrived shortly after her tea was ordered.

"We couldn't have conducted it better ourselves. My sources say that East Germany simply imploded on its foreign exchange balance of payments."

"Classic and consistent with our methods," Rock said.

"Exactly. Accident?"

"Sloppy, if it is."

"So you think someone is trying to get our attention?" Roth asked.

"Gentlemen, perhaps we are being paranoid. We aren't the only group capable of exerting power."

"Yes, but we either control or know about all the others. My concern is that I don't know who is behind this." Mr. Rock steepled his fingers.

"Perhaps we let it slide?" she said.

"Dangerous. If it is not an accident, they know who we are," Roth said.

"Or they believe they do."

"Do you think Getty talked?" Lady Teignmouth let the question hang, then took a sip of her tea. The others did the same. They had wondered about that since his murder almost fifteen years earlier.

"If he did, we'd all be dead."

"Who could have wanted him dead?"

"And make it look like an accident?"

"It only looked like an accident to those buffoons in the media. Everyone wanted him dead, so they looked the other way. I can't imagine the medical officers not raising suspicions."

"Especially with his guards dead nearby. Being in a basement clearly set up for torture wouldn't have helped."

"To be fair," Lady Teignmouth said, "I have fond memories of those rooms."

Both Rock and Roth took another sip of their tea. Neither wanted to think about that image.

"No need to be embarrassed," she continued. "I'm sure you two have your fair share of peccadilloes."

"We're not here to talk of such things, I'm sure," Rock said. "We need to determine whether our Order is at risk, and what to do about it."

"Can we find out who's behind the East Germany fiasco?"

"I have a name. A nobody, from what I can tell. Some banker."

"We can always use a good banker on our side," Roth said.

"Whispers are that he laundered drug money."

"And?"

"It is worth considering."

"Can he be acquired?" said Teignmouth.

"Probably. I don't have much on him."

"How can we make contact?"

"We don't," Rock said. "I don't want to risk us being dragged down into his personal tragedy of a life."

"Have him killed?"

"Unnecessary."

"Let him be?"

"Watch him. See what he does, who he's with, and who's against him."

"That's it?"

"For now. Get the FBI to monitor him. Maybe the DEA as well."

"And if he steps out of line?"

"He's expendable."

Chapter Seventeen

Square One

"We're back to square one, aren't we?"

Sylvia looked up from her computer. She enjoyed the power she held at her fingertips. "Never. We just need to find a new target. Something that will flush them out."

"Should we topple a bank? Another country?"

"Just because we got lucky once, doesn't mean it'll happen again."

Joe was nursing his coffee. He hunched his shoulders and leaned against his desk. "Maybe we were a little rough on George?"

Sylvia lost her smile. "That was disgusting. I hate myself for that."

"This is a tough business. There are no friendships."

"Even between us?"

"We're different."

"How?"

"You don't exist. There's no one to betray you."

"Except you," Sylvia said.

"Except me." He took another sip of his coffee.

"You know, George could still do a lot for us."

Joe didn't reply, but raised his eyebrows.

"He's got the infrastructure and credibility with the other banks. He still has a lot of money."

"I understand he got robbed," Joe said.

"What?" Sylvia let her hands drop from her keyboard and turned to face Joe directly. "Was he hurt?"

"Three gunshot wounds, a hundred million lighter, and a permanent cripple. I don't think he'll be looking to help us anytime soon."

"We had nothing to do with that."

Joe was silent.

"Did we?"

"No. We didn't do anything. Just bad luck. Some guy from the CIA, special division, wanted payback. Apparently, George has enemies."

Sylvia sat back in her chair, thoughtful. "Who would have thought? I always liked him, from the moment I met him."

"Then why betray him?" Joe asked, genuinely interested.

"Why'd he get robbed? Same reason."

"You're his enemy?"

"No," she said. "Weakness. People like him want to swim with sharks. They want to be above and below the law. They want, but aren't worthy."

"And you loved him."

Sylvia was silent. Joe knew how to push her buttons. Joe wasn't weak; he was scary. He was also the sexiest man she had ever met.

"You want to use him again?" she asked.

"Why break in a new horse when we already have one in the stable?"

"You're a bad man, Joe," she said. She got up and walked to him. She took his coffee and drank the rest. Standing, she unbuttoned her shirt and locked eyes with his.

"Sylvia, control yourself. I just want to drink my coffee in peace."

"You're a class 'A' sonofabitch, you know that?" She walked out, not bothering to button her shirt.

"And you're the only girl I've come close to loving since my wife, but that doesn't change the fact we need to get working on this."

Sylvia reappeared halfway through the door. Joe looked sideways at her and poured himself another coffee.

∞

"How long will we need to wait?"

"As long as it takes," Joe said.

"You hate them that much?"

"They are that dangerous."

Sylvia watched the snow that blanketed the city in silence, waiting for any movement to disturb the perfect scene. They had visited her parents in Montreal for

New Years and took a suite at the Ritz-Carlton. Part of her wanted to shock her parents with an old boyfriend. She succeeded on that front. However, once they started talking, the three became friendly. She feared him and wanted him all the more as a result.

"Maybe a frontal assault isn't the best when dealing with a group like the Order," she said. "If they are as powerful as you say, they have the security services, politicians, and financial muscle to do what they want. They will also learn of us, despite our caution."

"Our biggest asset is our size. We're too small to be noticed."

"I think they noticed East Germany."

"Which means we have their attention."

"Which means we need to step back and wait for their next move," she said.

"Yes, and dangle George. We agreed on that already."

Sylvia was silent for a moment. "We need someone who can monitor him close up. A romantic interest. That's his weakest point. He longs for a woman to tell him that she loves him and needs him."

"I've got the perfect specimen," Joe said with a smile. "It all depends whether he holds a grudge."

"If you mean who I think, you're crazy."

"Sometimes the most obvious is the best. They have already established a strong emotional bond."

"You can say that again." Sylvia climbed back under the covers and pushed herself next to Joe. "Some men can't resist a bad girl."

Chapter Eighteen

Rebuilding

"You're looking much better, son."

"I just wish I didn't have to deal with ice as well as gunshot wounds," George said.

"The doctor says you are doing remarkably well, and the shots didn't hit any bones in your shoulders."

"But it blew apart my knee. I'll never walk normally again."

George's father put his hand on his son's shoulder and didn't speak for a moment. "You're alive and I'm thankful for that."

George's eyes welled up despite himself. He wished he had his father's optimism in the face of defeat.

They looked up at the crunching of snow under tires. The vehicle was approaching slowly over the fresh snow. George was still on heavy pain medication for his injuries but tried to use his arms to support himself. It would have been comical if it wasn't so painful. They walked in the direction of the pickup truck. As the door opened, they could see who came out. George almost fell over with fear and his father froze.

"Jasmine," he hissed, almost letting go of his son.

"Hello, Mr. Anderson. George." She nodded to both.

"Came here to finish the job?" George said.

"I came here to seek your forgiveness."

"There's nothing to talk about."

"You know it's more complicated than that. Mr. Anderson, can I have a moment with your son?"

George's father looked at his son and felt as much as saw the nod. "I'm going to get my rifle. Don't try anything." He allowed her to take his place under George's arm.

"Don't worry, sir. I'm not going to hurt your son."

"Too late," he said as he walked away.

Jasmine and George watched the bundled figure walk through the white expanse. It wasn't far, but the fresh snow covered every branch, creating a winter wonderland. It was beautiful and breathtaking.

"Your father is quite the man," she said.

"What do you want, Jasmine?"

"Like I said, your forgiveness."

"Then what? You're going to rob me again?"

"I wish it could have been different. You know how it is. I love you, George. I always have and always will. I wish they never put me on those assignments."

"You're a good liar. I know that."

"Perhaps, but I'm not lying. Look into my eyes and you'll see that I'm telling the truth."

She turned towards him so he could see her face. Her hair was cut shorter, just longer than a bob, but still above her shoulders. Her face was still round, just older and more confident. Her eyes were surrounded by the softness of her skin that was just beginning to hint at wrinkles.

"All it shows is that you're an even better liar than I thought. You have figured out a way to lie to yourself."

"I know you're mad. I'm sorry I had to shoot you. You'll know I didn't mean to hurt you."

"Hurt me? How can you say that? I'll never walk properly again."

"They wanted me to kill you. They wanted me to torture you and extract the names of your clients, the techniques of your bank, and your involvement with the recent collapse of East Germany."

George was silent. Part of this rang true. He was guilty over his drug past and the mad people who laundered money through his structure, but we was proud of his involvement with the collapse of the Berlin Wall.

"So you took my money instead."

"It was General Calhoun's decision. Not mine."

George's head snapped back as though she had slapped him.

"Who?"

"General Calhoun. Why, do you know him?"

"How old is he?"

"I don't know, in his sixties."

"Did he serve in Vietnam?"

"I don't know. Most likely."

"The son of a bitch!" George wanted to punch something. "I knew it. The bastard was watching me all this time, just biding his time to take what he felt was his. He let me create the structure, take the chances, then scooped the cream at his convenience."

"What are you talking about?" Jasmine's face was etched with concern. This wasn't going as she planned. Her mission was to seduce, gain trust, and report back. Even dropping Calhoun's name was something she had cleared first with the general. She assumed George would check out her story. At no point did she imagine they already knew each other.

"He was my lieutenant in Laos."

"You mean Vietnam."

"No, I mean Laos. We were running heroin for the CIA to fund the rebels. I skimmed off the top. It was such a crazy time. No one noticed. Well, I thought no one noticed."

"Calhoun?"

"Yes. I wondered why everything went so smoothly. Every door was opened. I never had an argument or issue with the team. I was put in the front line with those power-mad Laotian generals. Now I know why. They never thought I'd survive."

"What are you saying?"

"Calhoun bided his time, then sent you to steal back the money I took."

"He said it was CIA money."

"Do you think the CIA saw any of it?"

"How did he get you the presidential pardon?"

"Maybe another division within the CIA. This was a black op. You don't just drop nearly a billion dollars onto the lap of the CIA director and say, 'wow, look what I found'. It would create more questions than answers. Peoples' heads would roll and careers end. Presidents know more than they pretend to. It's all about plausible deniability. The president gave the pardon because he knew the money would be redirected into a cause he supported."

Jasmine was silent. This was either above her security clearance, or he was paranoid. Perhaps that was why she was sent to observe him. It was a ballsy move to drive up to his parents' front door. *But*, she thought, *when did anything happen by being a coward?*

"What the hell is going on?" George said. He forgot the pain in his knee and his shoulders. The cold didn't help, but he needed to keep moving.

"I don't know," Jasmine said.

"And now you reappear? What do your masters have in store for me this time?"

"I volunteered."

"For what?"

"To come back and mend fences. I realized that I have loved you from the moment I met you in California in that beach café. I have never been loved back by anyone the way you loved me. I want that again."

George was silent but continued to fume. His anger was flowing towards Calhoun.

"I had no idea about Calhoun, George."

"How could you?"

"Exactly."

"But you were there to take the money."

"It was a mission. I didn't think I would feel so much for you. In some ways, I didn't want to believe them. It broke my heart when I discovered you had that kind of money. I wanted to live poor with you."

"Pretty words and well-rehearsed."

"You want to know why I took the assignment a few months ago?"

"The one where I was supposed to be killed?"

Jasmine ignored it. "I knew you had more. I thought that if I could just show them that you had value, I could keep you alive."

"By shooting me?"

"I was in a tight situation. Imagine if you were given a mission by the CIA to kill someone and you didn't. Does that make you a traitor? I had to injure you, and I had to bring back treasure to keep you alive."

George was silent. His world was shifting. He loved her once, but he didn't want to be a fool again. The hood on her jacket was down and her hair merged with the fur. It created a fuzzy corona around her face. She was no longer the monster he saw as she exited her truck; she was the girl who walked with her silk robe open as she made him breakfast. She was the hippie with ridiculous clothes who changed into a fashion icon when they reached New York. She was soft, the way he remembered Barbie. She was nothing like Sylvia's cold brilliance.

"George?" She touched him gently on the shoulder.

"I was just thinking about how we met and all the lies that you told me. I was happy with you."

"So was I. We were matched for compatibility. I laughed at the time, but it's true. I want us to have what your parents have. We are great together."

"As long as you aren't pointing a gun at me," he said with a slight smile.

"That's the George I remember." She was laughing now. "Give me your arm and we'll try to walk without the canes."

She put her arm around his waist when his arm proved too weak, and he put his around hers. She opened her jacket so she wasn't so bulky and he tucked his hand into her waistband. The walk was slow, but they made it to the end of the driveway before turning back and returning to the house.

"I think I should go," Jasmine said. She could see the sweat on his face from exertion.

"I'm glad it's not too cold or my face would be an icicle." George grimaced.

"I don't think your parents are ready to see me. Please send my regards to you mother."

She kissed George gently on his cheek. His hand was firmly on the rail next to the house. He watched her walk, obscured by the snow. He could still hear the crunch of her boots.

∞

Jasmine returned a few days later and they went for a drive. The temperature dropped and the winter wonderland was blown apart by wind, leaving naked trees and telephone lines. Roads were cleared and salted.

"Isn't it beautiful?" George said.

"George, have you been taking your medication?"

"I mean, the constancy of movement. The energy of people to overcome and continue despite the weather and circumstances. We go for a drive because we want to, not because we have to. We exert our will on our environment."

"Let me rephrase that," Jasmine said. "Have you been taking too many meds?"

George laughed. "I know I was wrong in what I did in Laos. Not the drug thing, the stealing thing. I deserved that. I should be happy I wasn't killed."

"Like you said, they wanted the money. They were probably impressed at how you pulled it off," she said.

"Maybe. Then I went and did the same thing again. I don't know how I didn't get shot by those madmen. You have no idea at how crazy they are. I've seen teenage boys killed for cleaning Rafa's car too much."

"Rafa?"

"The Medellin cartel's man on the ground in the US at the time. He was so paranoid, he thought that the boy was looking under his car to plant a bomb. He killed the boy, and another replaced him. No one said anything."

"Rough crowd."

"They made decisions while high on cocaine. They acted as though there was no consequence to their actions."

"And you feel you were like them?"

"Not like them, but I'm just as guilty. I didn't deserve the money I made. It was all tainted by blood."

Jasmine was silent.

"Everything I've done has either skirted the fringes of the law or was outright illegal. I got off lightly. Besides, if I wanted to have a last image in my head, it would be yours."

Jasmine felt his hand reach over and touch hers. She linked her fingers in his.

"I don't know if I'll ever trust you again, but I understand what you did." He stared in the distance and they drove without looking at each other.

"I was doing my job. It's all messed up, I know."

"Maybe."

They reached a crossroads and she slowed the truck.

"Which way do you want to go?"

Chapter Nineteen

Patriot

"She's in." Sylvia barely closed the door before starting to talk.

"Let's give her a long leash. I don't want to spook either of them." Joe rubbed his forehead, trying to remove an invisible spot.

"So we're playing matchmakers?"

"She may need to remain undercover for years. There's no certainty that the Order will approach him. All we did was put him on their radar. They're not stupid. They'll find out who he is. They are probably monitoring him as we speak."

"There's more. They may have already approached him."

Joe stopped rubbing his forehead and looked up.

"Someone pretending to be part of the CIA approached George to take down a shady bank. They say they want funding."

"What's going on over there? The CIA is becoming a bandit, stealing from one bad guy to fund their missions against others?"

"That is what the track record suggests," Sylvia said.

Joe didn't respond. His division of the CIA was secret to everyone. He was pleased to see the G29 spreading itself into top positions. Calhoun was a good and loyal member, and would be an ally in this fight. Regardless, Joe wasn't ready to let Calhoun know about this other group. He survived by keeping his cards close to his chest. He had told enough people and, so far, everyone he told had died.

"Anyway, the bank is controlled by a Pakistani and a Saudi. It's big, almost thirty thousand employees. Suspected of laundering money."

"Is this how they fund their black ops?"

"I don't know what they're doing. I am reporting what Jasmine has told us. This agent wants George to prove himself. They don't want to be involved in drugs, so they say, and are concerned that George is beholden to the cartels. They are demanding a show of loyalty."

"I'm not aware of anything like this happening at the CIA," Joe continued to mumble to himself. "I don't think this is genuine CIA. Any chance it is one of the Order's tentacles?"

"No way to know. George wants to do it. He wants to redeem himself. According to Jasmine, he is feeling guilty about the way he made his money and lived his life. He actually feels as though he deserved to be shot. By the end, he was crying in her arms asking her to forgive him. Her! I had no idea she was so good."

Joe had a faraway look in his eyes. "Dirty business, this. You never know what the truth is or who to trust. Remember that when I'm gone."

It was Sylvia's turn to be alarmed. "Where are you going?"

"I'm not going to live forever, am I? Don't worry, I'm not going anywhere just yet."

Sylvia put her hands on his face and kissed him until he needed to breathe. She held him close to her. He had become her life, controlling her like no man she had ever known. His strength gave her comfort and fear in equal measures.

"I don't know when he's going to act. Whoever contacted him will provide him with the information. They want deniability. I guess we'll see what happens."

"We won't be purely passive. I want daily reports," Joe said. "This is your responsibility. You run Jasmine. Don't tell her anything; she must tell you. I'm only trusting you and I expect you to only trust me. Something stinks but I can't put my finger on it."

"I trust you." She said it like a little girl. She wanted to make love to him right there and then.

"We can't get sentimental. I'll stay in touch with Calhoun. Watch your back and make sure he doesn't know we're spying on his agent."

"I'll do my part."

"I know you will." Joe allowed her hands to trace his body. He kissed her gently and picked her up. He still had the strength of his youth in his sixty-year-old body.

∞

It took longer than any of them thought before BCCI was taken down. George liked the symmetry of destroying the bank he recommended to the Colombian cartels. It was finally raided by officials on 5 July 1991. The money he needed to take was already long gone. The Pakistani and Saudi would be blamed, but he was the cause.

"I thought Berlin was going to be my crowning achievement," George said. "But this feels better. With Berlin, I didn't understand all of the machinations going on behind the scenes. I was bait. This time, I am doing something good for the country."

"Yes, baby. You're the best." Jasmine wrapped her arms around him and kissed his neck. "I don't know what the CIA or any of them would do without you."

"Flattery will get your everywhere." George registered the sarcasm, but dismissed it as her quirky way of talking. It excited him to have her next to him, praising him.

"Is there anywhere I haven't been?"

"I guess we'll need to find out."

There was a knock on the door and they ignored it. The knock came again.

"Sorry, Jas. Let me see who that jackass is. Who the hell is bothering us here?"

He got up, put on his robe, and went to the door. "Who is it?"

"Open up. Police."

George cracked the door and saw two officers in uniform. They weren't smiling. He opened the door wide.

"Can I help you, officers?"

"Are you George Anderson?"

"Yes?"

"I have something for you."

The second officer, behind the one who talked, handed George a package wrapped in brown paper and tied with twine.

"What is it?"

"No idea. I'm just delivering it."

"From whom?"

"I don't know that either. I'm just following orders."

"Thank you, officer. Anything else?"

The officer caught a peek into the hotel room and saw a reflection of Jasmine in the mirror. "Nothing, sir. Have a good evening."

"I will. You too."

George closed the door and began turning the package over in his hands.

"Who was that, sweetie?"

"Police. Delivering packages. Surreal."

The package was bulky and soft. He took it into the sitting area of his suite and found a knife.

"Do you need any help?"

"No, I think I'm okay. Curiosity has gotten the better of me."

"Be careful, George." Jas was naked as she walked into the room. She snuggled in behind him and looked over his shoulder.

He used the knife to cut the twine and unwrapped the paper carefully. "I hope it's not a bomb."

"If it is, we're screwed, so don't worry. On second thought, I'll get some champagne from the other room while you open it."

George turned around and kissed her. Seeing her naked, he took off his robe and wrapped her in it. He sat down, brown paper on the coffee table, and wondered what to do next.

"I guess we can't be squeamish now." He flipped the paper over and continued unwrapping it. He saw black, then a flash of white.

"Is that what I think it is?" Jas was almost laughing.

"I think so. A tux. What the hell?"

"There's a note stuck in the pocket. Here. You read it."

George felt the quality of the bonded paper and read the words.

"What's it say?" Jas said.

"I've been invited to a party."

"Great. Which one? I'll get ready."

"It says that I am to go alone."

"Who cares what the note says?"

"I do when it's delivered by the police and it involves meeting the chairman of the Federal Reserve."

∞

The formal gathering was at the Rockefeller Center. George was surprised when the tuxedo fit him perfectly. In a daze, he took a taxi to the event. He showed his ticket and was let in. The gigantic proportions of the room set out in art deco dwarfed the great and the good within. He only needed to find one of them.

Alan Greenspan was tall and would likely have a crowd surrounding him at all times, he figured. He was the wunderkind who floated to the top of the financial regulators and held the reigns of the most powerful central bank in the world. For whatever reason, he had the confidence of the powers of the land. *Safe pair of hands*, George thought.

"No, thank you." George waved away the champagne. He wanted to see what this was about. It didn't take him too long to find the chairman.

"Excuse me, Mr. Greenspan?" George wondered at the meekness in his voice.

The famous bespectacled man turned around and George could see all of his acolytes turn with him. All eyes faced him.

"Yes? May I help you?" His glasses filled half his face and enlarged his eyes.

"My name is George Anderson. I received a message that you wanted to talk to me."

A shadow passed over his face but he recovered quickly. Anyone watching closely would put it down to his intense intellect and impatience for petty interruptions.

"Yes, I remember." He turned to those around him. "I'll need a moment. We'll continue this later. Thank you." He returned to George and extended his hand. "Nice to finally meet you, Mr. Anderson."

"It is an honor to meet you, sir."

"Let's find a corner where we can talk. Did you have any trouble getting here?"

George tried not to laugh. "If the taxi couldn't find this venue, he should be fired."

"True enough. We should be out of earshot here."

The room was filled with orchestral music, diamonds, and beautiful people. It was a regular event in the calendar of the twelve Federal Reserves, but the man everyone looked to, who controlled the whole system, was facing George. The chairman was the final word and, despite the voting system, he carried a lot of weight. In the vast majority of instances, votes were unanimous.

"I'm in the dark, Mr. Greenspan. How can I help you?"

Greenspan paused, removed his glasses, and rubbed the bridge of his nose. He held his glasses by one of its arms.

"I've been instructed to inform you that you are now part of the Treasury. I understand that you would be best placed within the international affairs division. That should give you the freedom of movement and access you'll need." He put his glasses back on.

"I don't understand, sir. I didn't apply for the job."

"Since when has that ever been an impediment to a career?" he snapped. Then he regained his composure. George had never heard of him losing his temper like that. "You people think that the rest of us don't matter. As though you can dictate your will regardless of what is best for the country?"

"Sir?"

"Don't play dumb with me. I'm not wearing a wire. No one is listening."

"Sir, thank you for the job, but I really don't know what you're talking about."

"If you want to continue your fiction, that's your business, Mr. Anderson. My job is to bring you in from the cold. That's a direct quote, mind you. They wanted me to tell you that."

"They?"

Greenspan ignored the question. "Your position is special within the Treasury. There are the normal functions, but you will be free to undertake special investigations and develop a team under you. Your hands are free. You will have the credibility to do what you want, and the resources to carry it out successfully."

George looked at him as though he had grown a second head.

"There is one condition, however," Greenspan said. "I am told that your girlfriend is a spy. You are to stop seeing her immediately."

"Jasmine? A spy?" George knew it was true, but he had crossed the line of reason long ago.

Greenspan looked pained. "This isn't my forte. I'm a banker, not a spy. I really find these assignments distasteful. I've been told that you have been of great assistance to the country; that you're a patriot. I applaud you. I also understand that this position is one of redemption. I don't want to know what that means. Are we clear?"

"Understood, sir. "

"If you'll excuse me, I need to mingle before they start to talk. Come by the office first thing next week. We'll have your office ready by then."

"Thank you, sir."

"Oh, and one more thing. We don't talk, understood? This is a one-off. For some reason, they wanted to impress you. I hope it worked."

∞

They. The word rang in George's ear the rest of the evening. It turned to poison as he returned to his room. He understood the demand intellectually, but the thought of losing Jasmine after everything they'd been through was weighing heavily on him.

"How did your meeting with God go?" Jasmine was irritated.

"Fine. Bizarre. I don't know."

Jasmine kissed him as he entered their suite. She took his jacket and began unbuttoning his clothes.

"Let's get you out of this monkey suit."

George put his hands on hers. "I have something to tell you."

She stopped fidgeting and took a step backwards. As usual, her robe was open in the front and she was reassured by George's eyes.

"I've been offered a top job, but it comes with conditions. One of them is that 'they', whoever they are, do not want you next to me. They think you are a spy."

"Of course I'm a spy. I've never made a secret of that. We both know that."

"I know. That's what makes this so shitty."

"Poor Georgie. I know you want to do the right thing." She was next to him again, her hand on his face.

"I'm thinking about turning the job down. We've come so far, been through so much, it would be crazy to abandon us."

"George, I know this is what you want to do. I want you to do this too. You tell me that you have nightmares of your past. This is a chance to redeem yourself. Do something purely because it's the right thing to do."

"And us? Aren't we worth fighting for?"

"Of course we are, but if we are having this conversation, I think you are struggling with the decision.

There shouldn't be a struggle. If there is, then take the job."

She kissed him lightly on his cheek and he could feel her tears on his skin when she walked away. He let her go. She was right. All he ever wanted was to belong and to be recognized for who he was. He wasn't a traitor, he was a patriot. This was a step towards proving it.

Chapter Twenty

Joe

"We've lost her."

"What do you mean?"

"George was approached by Alan Greenspan, if you can believe it, and was told that he needed to dump Jasmine."

"And in return?"

"He gets a plum job in the Treasury. Some special position that allows him freedom of movement and excellent cover."

"So the Order has made their move and they are using George as their pawn." Joe was smiling. "This is excellent news."

"But we lost our eyes and ears," Sylvia said.

"Temporarily. Let's see how things go."

"Are we shut down temporarily?"

"I don't think so. Monitor things the best you can. You keep saying how you like hacking. Make yourself at home in the government systems. See what passes on the wire from our dear Mr. Anderson. Things don't work quickly with these people. Everything is measured in years. If they are moving this pawn, they have some major play in mind, possibly years away."

"Who do you think?"

"They move against countries. We only need to look at those countries not already in their thrall."

"You mean all countries not firmly ensconced with the IMF and other international agencies?"

"If a country can't borrow money, then the Order can't exert control over it. Ask yourself why countries are so terrified of defaulting."

"They can't borrow more."

"Exactly. Fear keeps them in line. Most countries are intelligent enough to know that they are either currently insolvent or a few bad quarters away from it. They constantly need to have easy credit available to them. Without it, they starve and die."

"Or go to war."

Joe smiled again. "But few are brave or crazy enough to do that."

"Except the US, Russia, and China."

"And the US is definitely part of the game, so, it is either Russia or China."

"China is too independent and possibly too vulnerable to allow itself to be entangled by the siren call of western finance and its terms. I would guess Russia."

"I agree," Joe said. "Which means this will be a multi-year plan. This operation goes into a holding pattern. I have been threatening retirement for a while. Perhaps I'll try it for a bit. We can remain in touch, but I think it best if we don't see each other for a while."

Sylvia felt like she had been punched in the gut. Her hand instinctively began rubbing her solar plexus. "What are you saying, Joe?"

"We've had a good run. Now it's over."

"I thought you loved me."

Joe's head dropped and he exhaled. "Sylvia, I do love you, but you're thirty years younger than me. You'll want a family and a normal husband."

"I don't want a normal husband, I want you." She was crying and her skin became blotchy with red.

"I'll take that as I should," Joe said, "but I've seen how this ends. People around me die. Let me love you by leaving you."

Sylvia put herself into his arms. "I won't."

Joe stroked her hair and whispered softly into her ear. He knew these things took time, but leaving was inevitable.

∞

Six months later, Joe moved into his non-descript house in a small American town in the middle of nowhere. He made sure his garage was outfitted with tools to keep himself busy. He always loved working with his hands, even though he was considered a genius when he was in school. He never found any use for his brain, although it probably kept him alive despite all the things he had done in his life.

G29 stationed him there. He would always be on call, he knew that. His past could never be erased and he could never forget. Sylvia was a minor distraction, however sweet. He thought about living out his days with her and could only feel the pain from the loss of his wife, their child Isabella, and the life he imagined with them. He had enemies and bad luck. It was not the type of world he wanted to invite Sylvia into. She would be better off on her own. With her looks and brain, he reasoned, she wouldn't be alone long.

His new home looked like something out of a classic fifties American sitcom. There was nothing to complain about. The streets were wide with well-established trees. The houses were set back far from the road, and from each other. He had money, lots of it, but the idea of living out his life in anonymity was priceless.

Sylvia came to visit at first. They would revert to becoming animals for the first few days as they exhausted their sexual needs. Then, they would walk through the town holding hands. There was nothing else to do. He loved it. She didn't. Eventually, the visits became less frequent and the bond began to sever. They both loved each other, but she knew he had a past that couldn't be tamed. She also knew that he would never be hers.

"Mr. Steinberger? Yes, sorry, you forgot your bag."

Joe turned and retrieved his missing grocery bag. "Thank you. I'd lose my head if it wasn't screwed on."

"You're such a kidder," the red-faced cashier said. She was blushing as she studied his face.

"Have a nice day," Joe said and walked out of the automatic doors and towards his house. It wasn't far and he enjoyed walking. When he had cleared the parking lot, he began laughing. "You've got a wicked sense of humor," he said to himself.

It was a stroke of genius. He was a single man in his sixties moving into a small town. He knew that everyone would talk, so he gave them something to talk about.

"Tell them I don't want to talk to the press," he had said into a payphone. He knew there were people within earshot and put on a good performance.

"No, I'm not the bastard son of Albert Einstein. Tell them they've got their facts wrong. Tell them I just want to be left alone."

"No, I don't want to give an interview to that effect."

"No, I won't tell you where I'm living."

"Okay, trace the call. Do your worst. I'm hanging up."

As he turned around, every head was looking elsewhere—reading the bulletin board, getting a Coke from the vending machine, talking with their neighbor.

Good, he thought. *Mission accomplished.*

Within a week, everyone in town knew the bastard son of Albert Einstein was hiding out in their little town. He was a celebrity. No one ever mentioned this to his face or enquired after him. He was given every courtesy allowed to his privacy.

A year passed since the loss of Jasmine and their mission. He didn't worry. He now had a definite link to the Order. No one else could have engineered it so quickly and with such prominent players.

Two years passed and Sylvia began slipping away. She came less frequently and didn't cry during the last visit. It was five years before he saw the fruits of George's actions but, by then, his life had become complicated.

He was shopping for his groceries, as he did every week, at the same mall that was within walking distance of his home. In the supermarket, a woman approached him.

"Hi," she said. "I don't think we've met. I'm Denise and my husband James is just down aisle four. We're neighbors, well, on the same street." She was babbling and tried to force her mouth shut.

"Nice to meet you, ma'am," Joe said.

"We only moved to town a year ago and our work keeps us so busy we don't have much extra time to socialize. I feel terrible that we haven't met and talked before this."

"I've seen you both around. I remember you because you hold hands when you walk. You also leave

for work around seven in the morning in a blue Ford."
Joe noticed her looking at him. "It's a small town and
I like to watch people," he said by way of explanation.
"It's better than TV."

"Now I feel even guiltier," she said.

James joined them and introduced himself. They
shook hands.

"Say, do you want to join us for dinner tonight?
We're making a roast with all the trimmings."

Joe hesitated. "Sure. I'd love to. When do you want
me to drop by?"

"Arrive at 6:30 for drinks and we'll eat around
seven. Is that too late for you?"

"No, it's perfect. Can I bring anything?"

"Absolutely not, Mr. Steinberger."

"Please, call me Joe."

It took a few meals, but he eventually learned of the
reason behind them approaching him. It perpetuated
his cover story. They wanted the DNA from one of the
most brilliant scientists in history. Joe assured them
that he wasn't brilliant, only the bastard son of one.
They didn't seem to care. They couldn't have children,
and Joe became the father of their child through artifi-
cial insemination.

Jack was born as the debt negotiations between
Russia and the Paris and London Clubs were completed in 1997. The clubs were formed to help
sovereign countries deal with their debt burdens more
effectively. Between them, the International Monetary

Fund, and the global speculators, countries were at the mercy of outsiders. This was the playground of the Order.

"He is the most beautiful boy," Joe said. He had tears in his eyes as he remembered Isabella and his dead wife. Jack was wrapped in blue with a blue cap on his head. Joe held him like the most precious thing in the world.

"Thank you, Joe," Denise said. Her face was puffy from tears and exhaustion.

"We'd like you to be godfather to Jack, if you are okay with that?" James was proud and excited but seemed awkward around the biological father of his son.

"It would be my greatest honor. You have made me a very happy man."

"You have made us happier than we both deserve," James said. He clasped Joe on the back.

We can be a family, Joe thought. It made him want to forget all of his old missions. He wanted out. The Order would not be taken down by him. It was no longer his fight.

∞

"Seven years and you give up like this?" Sylvia was fuming. "I thought we had a mission."

"I told you, people die when they get close to me."

Sylvia saw that she was making no impact. She changed tactics. "We tried over three years for our own. I loved you. I thought you loved me. But there was no baby. There never would be."

Joe tried not to be affected. He knew she was capable of manipulation. He wasn't looking for a baby, even if she was. He always assumed she was on the pill.

"Do you need to do that?"

She didn't say anything. She slipped out of bed towards the bathroom. He heard the water running. He turned over and tried to enjoy the moment. For anyone else, it would be heaven.

"I have to go," she said.

Joe grunted, then inhaled deeply and exhaled. He didn't want to talk.

"It was fun," she said.

"Hmm."

"Can I see you again?"

"Yeah." He wished she would shut up.

He felt her body against him, trying to find a place on his face to kiss. He felt her lips against him and the cold of her wet hair.

"Tonight?"

He nodded and watched her gather her clothes. Within ten minutes, she had left and he was alone. *At least I have Jack*, he thought, and went to sleep.

Chapter Twenty-One

Welcome to the Club

"Mr. Rock, it is a pleasure and a great privilege to meet you," George said. They were in the vault room of the Trinity Place Bar and Restaurant.

"The pleasure is all mine. I hope you don't mind the location. It allows my people to ensure it is secure while we talk."

"This is a great place. I've heard of it before but never had a reason to come."

"I've been watching your career and hearing things about you."

George raised his eyebrows. "All good things, I hope?"

"I wouldn't be here if they weren't." Rock ignored George's past and had no intention of raising it. It was ancient history.

"How can I help you, Mr. Rock?"

"Did you ever wonder how you received help with the BCCI affair? Or why you were approached?"

George was silent. "I don't ask questions when good things happen, sir."

"Or how you got the job at Treasury?"

"That was eerie. Again, I have been around long enough to know that some things do not go from A to B. Sometimes, Z follows A."

"I like that. Exactly. I've been involved in a few men's careers that have gone like that."

George was silent. He figured he could guess a few of those men.

"What I'm here to talk to you about today is not a career, but a calling."

"Sir?"

"I am part of a small group of people who are fiercely private and who aim to bring order to the world."

"A think tank?"

"A bit more than that. It is a group where people do things. It is not only talk."

"Sounds intriguing."

"There is a catch."

"There always is, isn't there, sir?"

"You need to join blind and you can't leave. We take our secrets seriously."

George digested this. "Then I have no decision. If you are part of the group and people aren't allowed to leave, then I must join or face the consequences as though I had betrayed the group."

"Smart boy. I knew you'd figure that out. Just in case, let me make this clear. We are not a conspiracy or a cabal. We are concerned people who make a difference. We don't care what political party you belong to or what you've done in the past to make your billions. We don't pay, we don't have staff, and we don't take notes."

The yellow light created a warm glow with the brass and stone in the room. It made Mr. Rock's eyes fiery.

"Then how is anything achieved?"

"We know people," he said, sitting back. "People with influence. They control other people with influence."

"Are they all part of the same group?"

"They are unaware of any group. It is a whisper, an order, or the view from the wrong end of a gun. Different people need different means of persuasion. We don't concern ourselves with those things. We are concerned about the macro, the global, and the vision."

"I don't fully understand. Why would you want me? I'm not an industrialist. I'm barely a billionaire. I don't have the people underneath me that you might assume."

"No. You're an unusual pick, but you're a patriot. You're a doer. You helped the CIA using unconventional methods during the Vietnam War. You helped the Colombians with their problems. You did all of this while protecting yourself and acting within the law. You gained a conscience and helped topple one of history's greatest tragedies."

"The Berlin Wall?"

"Yes, and then the USSR itself. All achieved using money no one is supposed to even know about. You did what our group does, but almost all alone. I know you had help and we assisted in our way. The CIA and that girlfriend of yours were there, but you were the one. While the world was worried about nuclear weapons and Russia's disarmament, you were diligently working on a way to trap the Soviets and squeeze it when it was weakest."

"That was you helping me," George said.

"But you have seen behind the curtain. Most never get that privilege. They moan and complain and fear, but rarely act. You saw the way Asia moved against the ruble. Instead of trying to fight the forces of capitalism, you directed it. You helped create the perfect storm that brought the once-mighty and independent Russia to her knees."

Rock's lips were white with spittle. He drank some water and wiped his mouth. George waited before speaking.

"Then the United States and IMF came up with a rescue package that saved Russia and put everything back to square one," George said.

"That's where you lost the plot, Mr. Anderson. That's where we finally seized control. That's also why you no longer need to continue your attack on Russia."

"You wanted them saved? Then why make them collapse?"

"We want them to flourish, like we want all countries to flourish, but under certain conditions. They need to integrate their financial systems of debt and trade with ours. Then, they play their games with our rules. We don't want to rule the world, only set the rules everyone else follows."

"And in so doing," George said, "control the world."

Rock smiled and stood. "Welcome to the club, Mr. Anderson. We'll be in touch."

George stood and shook his hand. He watched as the elderly man was engulfed by his security guards and disappeared around the corner. Looking around, he remembered where he was. *I'll drink to that*, he thought.

∞

So Joe was right, George thought. *And he wants them dead. He'll probably want me dead too, or tortured.* He shuddered. Jon Roberts and the cocaine smugglers seemed reasonable compared to the people he was mingling with now.

"Mr. Anderson?"

"Yes. Present."

George didn't understand why they took roll call if minutes weren't kept. Or perhaps, there were minutes and it was another deception. The higher he went, the less certainty he had of those around him.

"Welcome to our newest member." Lady Teignmouth was chairing the meeting. They were gathered in Rome for the signing of a treaty to create a permanent International Criminal Court. It was the type of cover that its members could use to meet in secret. "Is there any new business?"

The meeting went as George anticipated. He didn't say a word. Mr. Rock and Mr. Roth dominated discussions ranging from the new Euro to the dream of a global currency. Tributes were made to the passing of great leaders, and the group broke up for the evening. None of the members stuck around to mingle. Within an hour, George was alone, wondering where he was going to go for dinner.

The day was long and finally cooling by the time he left Cavalieri, the Waldorf Astoria Hotel in Rome. As he stepped onto Via Alberto Cadlolo, a man put a hood on his head from behind and he heard the screeching of tires. He felt his body thrown into the back of a vehicle and the sound of the engine screaming as it shifted through its gears. He felt rough hands tie his feet and wrists together.

"I guess I knew you were coming," he said, strangely calm. His voice was muffled by the hood.

There was no reply.

"You can tell Joe that this isn't necessary."

All he felt was the cobblestones under the tires and the occasional speedbump taken too fast. It caused him to rise off the floor and slam back down.

"You can tell Sylvia that I forgive her. It's in her nature."

The vehicle took a hard turn and he rolled on the floor.

"I'm not saying anything, so you may as well kill me now." He had an inspiration and felt this was the best way to deal with kidnappers. If he took their oxygen away, their will would be extinguished.

Again, only silence.

He began to feel the ridges in the floor and the wheel well. He tried to get comfortable, pushing himself against the wall so that he wasn't thrown around like a rag doll. The speed didn't abate and anxiety rose within him. His mind accelerated and had conversations with himself. With others. Skeletons of enemies past cantered in the space of his mind. The trip wasn't ending. His stomach ached from the tension of his unexercised torso. He wasn't out of shape, but these were muscles he didn't know he used or needed.

The vehicle stopped suddenly and he heard the sound of small pebbles under the tires. The engine was shut off and the doors opened. He heard the distinctive sliding of a van door and felt two sets of rough hands on him again. He was dragged, led, and pushed to his destination.

When the hood came off, he was in a room of light. There were four spotlights facing him, making everything invisible past their glare. The lights encircled him and were placed a little too close. He could feel the heat off their bulbs. His legs were tied to the chair but his hands were free. He ran his fingers through his hair and shielded his eyes from the light.

"Hello?"

Silence.

"What am I supposed to do? What do you want me to say?"

He couldn't sense anyone in the room with him. He heard the sound of a door opening, footsteps, and a door closing.

"Mr. Anderson?"

"Yes."

"I'm sorry to meet you under these circumstances, but I am sure you will agree that I had no choice."

"Who are you?"

"You know."

"I don't."

"Think harder."

George wracked his brain. Colombians? Pissed off bankers? Pissed off Russians? Joe?

"I don't know what you want from me." His voice shook a little, betraying the inevitable.

"I want information."

George felt a cold trickle of sweat, despite the lamps.

"Banking information?"

"Information on your new friends."

"I don't have any friends."

"On that, we agree."

"I have money. I can give you money. Just don't kill me."

"We'll take that too. Thank you."

"Okay. You can have my money. I don't have anything else you want."

"Are you happy?"

"What?"

"I said, are you happy?"

"Who the hell is happy? What has that got to do with anything?"

"You're rich. You've had beautiful women. You've had power. You must be happy."

"I don't have money. You just took it. All the women in my life have betrayed me. And any power I may have had is over as soon as you kill me."

"So you have nothing to lose. Tell me everything you know."

"I don't know anything."

"It'll make you happy."

"Are you insane? Just kill me. I can see you want to torture me."

There was silence, then the sound of footsteps, and the door closing.

Chapter Twenty-Two

Interrogation

An hour passed and no one returned. George began to feel the need to use the toilet.

"Hello! Hello! I need to go to the can!" He had always used the term. It was something he picked up from his father.

There was nothing for a few minutes, then the click of the door opening, footsteps, and the door closing. George's eyes could only see black spots as he crushed his eyes shut against the light.

"Tell us something first."

"I have nothing to say. I don't know why you're doing this to me. I'm just a businessman."

"No one is just anything. You know that better than most. Now tell me, Mr. Anderson. Tell me anything and I'll let you go to the can, as you so eloquently put it."

George was silent. He could picture his face browning as though he was inside a tanning salon. He smirked at the image.

"Do you find me funny, Mr. Anderson? Did I say something amusing?"

"No, sir. I was thinking about… nothing. Just a stupid image in my head."

"Tell me about it."

"It was nothing."

"I will let you pee if you tell me."

"I was thinking that the lights are like a tanning salon. It made me chuckle at the absurdity of the thought in this situation."

"Good. That's very good. That wasn't difficult, was it?"

"No, sir. Thank you. I really appreciate you letting me go."

"Who said anything about letting you go anywhere? I said I would allow you to pee. Now, go ahead."

"Here?"

"There's nothing to be embarrassed about, Mr. Anderson. You will see that things become a lot more intimate as this conversation continues."

The lights were beginning to make George's mind ache. He could only think about the lights. Then, he thought about his suit and allowed himself to release his bladder. He waited for it to flow, but it wouldn't. He tried to relax, but it was impossible. His mind wouldn't let him piss his own pants voluntarily. He laughed.

"I see you are enjoying yourself, Mr. Anderson. I hope that I will continue to entertain you. I also see that you have changed your mind about relieving yourself. It is funny how the mind sometimes doesn't co-operate. Let's hope for your sake that it stops listening to you and allows you to start talking."

George heard the familiar steps and the door closing. The next time he heard those same sounds, he was beginning to feel drowsy. He couldn't determine how long it had been since the last talk.

"Mr. Anderson, please drink this. I don't want you to die from dehydration."

George drank it. As he swallowed, he remembered a technique used by interrogators where they would make the victim drink something to cause diarrhea. "Too late to regret that," he said partly to himself.

"What's that, Mr. Anderson? Please speak up."

"I was just commenting to myself that it was too late to regret drinking that."

"Don't worry. We're not going to kill you like that. Yes, you guessed right. It'll take a little while. You'll embarrass yourself and it'll smell something awful, but we'll be on our first step towards getting some answers. And you want answers, don't you?"

"What do you want with me? Kill me, ransom me, or rob me. I don't have anything else."

"I beg to differ. Let's play a game. I'll say some words and you say the first thing that pops into your mind, okay?"

"Do I have a choice?"

"Obviously not."

"Can I say something before we begin?"

"Yes, that's why we're here. I do wish you would allow us to talk like gentlemen and get this over with."

"When your father was raping you as a child, did you mother watch? Did your sister eat popcorn? Or perhaps she was recording it?"

"Very funny, Mr. Anderson. Ha ha. I'll thank you for not regressing to that level of interaction. It demeans us both."

George was silent.

"Let's begin. CIA."

"Government," George said.

"Laos."

"Hot."

"Vietnam."

"Very hot."

"Calhoun."

"Asshole."

"Drugs."

"Cocaine."

"Heroin."

"Money."

"Money."

"Drugs."

"Rock."

"Scissors."

"Roth."

George paused.

"Faster, Mr. Anderson. This is a test."

"Wealthy."

"Teignmouth."

"Power."

"President."

"Puppet."

"Guns."

"Roses."

"Very funny, Mr. Anderson. I think we'll stop it there. You've done well. You've been most instructive."

He was left alone again. When he could hold it no longer, George released his bowels and bladder. His seat became greasy with feces and he could feel it run down his leg. The smell wasn't as bad as he anticipated, but something in him broke.

The heat from the lamps made it worse. As he had already shat himself, he pushed so that everything was out. Urine puddled around him and he became aware that his chair was secured to the floor. The gaps in his pant legs filled with the diarrhea and the image was more disturbing than the embarrassment.

When the door opened again, he heard a new sound. It was the sound of the lights moving closer to him. The heat intensified and he became nervous of becoming blind.

"Hey!" He felt someone grab his arms and cried out involuntarily. They were pulled tight and tied behind him.

"Comfortable, Mr. Anderson?" The voice of his interrogator never rose above conversation level. It was calm and reassuring at all times.

"I've been better, thanks for asking."

"Tsk, tsk. Don't get like that. I thought we were really getting somewhere on the last exercise."

"I don't know anything."

"So you keep telling me. My assistant will help me with the next phase. Please stay still, will you?"

A man with a black mask came into view as a shadow. George wasn't able to open his eyes but he felt his presence. He tried to open his eyes but the pain was too great. The constant red behind his eyelids had become black long ago.

The man grabbed his legs and used scissors to cut the length of the pant leg up to his crotch. George flinched but controlled himself the best he could. The man did the same with the other pant leg.

"I can see you don't mind shit on your hands," George said.

The man didn't respond. He used scissors to cut off George's underwear, exposing his genitals.

George felt a cold fear grip him. Then he realized that the lights were being moved backwards. His body relaxed, despite the situation.

The man took more rope and tied George's legs to the back of the chair to ensure that they were spread open and he could access the genitals without any interference by George. He heard a strange new sound and smelled something like burning metal.

"You can open your eyes now, Mr. Anderson. The lights should be far enough back. I want you to see this."

George allowed his eyelids to relax and slowly opened them. It was still bright but not painful. He saw the hooded man with two probes, like the ends of a car battery charger. He touched them together and they sparked. It created the metal smell.

"Before we go further, let me ask you some more questions."

George stared at the probes. The interrogator was invisible to him.

"How do you know Mr. Rock and Mr. Roth?"

"Through magazines, television articles. They are well known."

"I don't believe you. I think you are acquainted with them both."

"I have never met them. Sorry."

"Think carefully, Mr. Anderson. Have you ever heard of a secretive club, or perhaps you are a member of such a club?"

"Like the Jehovah's Witnesses? They're not that secretive. Just ask them. They'll be happy to talk your ear off."

"Again with the humor. Very funny. Let me ask another question. Do you know a woman named Jasmine? Very pretty girl."

George wasn't expecting her in the conversation and his mind whipsawed. "Yes." He had no reason to lie.

"You know that she is a spy?"

"Yes."

"And that she has had your son?"

George forgot about the probes and feces and lights. "What? You're lying. I would have heard."

"Did you give her a chance? You were in such a hurry to climb the ladder, to redeem yourself. Don't you ever think about those you stepped on while on the way up?"

George turned in on himself. Jas was damaged goods. She shot him, betrayed him. Why should he care about her? "I didn't know," he said.

"Let me enlighten you," he purred. He knew he had finally found a soft spot. "I'm going to ask you more questions. If you don't tell me the truth, I'll visit your whore of a girlfriend and dismember her slowly. As I'm sure she doesn't know what you know, I'll probably end up killing her before getting the information I need. Then, I'll have to turn to your baby boy."

"Enough!" George cried. "Just kill me. You're going to do it anyway."

"Tell me who is in the Order. Don't worry about all the names. Just one. If you give me one name, I'll let you go."

George knew how this went. It wasn't that different from torture in Laos and Vietnam. He was a dead man. It was his choice whether he died a coward or with honor.

"Go fuck yourself."

"I'll take that as a no, thank you."

He nodded and the hooded man walked towards George and tapped the two probes together, showering him with sparks. He then attached the ends and George felt the metal bite into his most sensitive skin, or at least that was how it felt.

"Thank you for being gentle when you put those on," George managed between gritted teeth. He braced himself for the current. He didn't know how he would react. He was glad he had already shat himself. If he hadn't, he would be now.

"Mr. Anderson, you have proven yourself a strong man. Much stronger than I gave you credit for when I first came in. From my research, I gathered that you would break."

"Does that mean you're letting me go?"

"Oh, we both know how this ends. You will die fast or slow. The choice is yours."

George slumped in his chair. He suspected but was afraid of this.

"But don't despair, Mr. Anderson. I have another game for you and me. You must agree that games are important to help break the tedium of the daily grind."

George was silent.

"Igor, give him the gun on the table. Yes, now untie his hands. Good. Mr. Anderson, that gun has one bullet. You can choose to do with it as you want. You can try to shoot poor Igor but he hasn't done anything wrong to you. He's just doing his job. You can try to shoot me, but I would guess that you wouldn't kill me. You'd maim me at best. These lights do have their uses."

"Or I can kill myself." George grabbed the gun off the table.

"No! Don't do it, Mr. Anderson."

"Go fuck yourself."

He pulled the trigger.

Chapter Twenty-Three

Success

George felt the click of the hammer being released. Everything in his life slowed down. He thought about Jasmine and the newborn baby he would never see. He thought about Sylvia and how they took on the Colombian cartels. He saw himself alone at the top of the Empire State Building waiting for Barbie. She would never come.

Click.

George's senses collapsed as his body shook from adrenaline. He felt hands untying him and carrying him somewhere.

"Am I dead? Is this heaven?"

There was no response. He saw a room all in white with a woman, also in white. She had a kind face and was talking to him. He couldn't hear her. He saw her take something and put it around him. It was soft, like a blanket or robe. He saw a shower with water already running. He was put into it, fully clothed, with the woman. She began unbuttoning his clothes and washing him. All the dirt, feces, and urine was washed away. She was gentle and he shook like a little boy. When he was clean, he was led out of the shower into a new white robe. Another woman took him to an adjoining room.

Seated in the room were Mr. Rock and Mr. Roth. He was seated across from them in an overstuffed leather chair. They were smoking cigars and he was offered one. Not a word had been spoken. A measure of scotch was poured into a glass and handed to him.

"I think it's your favorite fifty-year old scotch," Rock said. He lifted his glass towards George.

"What the hell is happening here?" George said. "I don't give a fuck about some shitty piss in a glass or cigar. I was tortured."

"Hazing. We've all been through it. Because we value our secrecy, we take it a little further than most."

"You think?"

"Don't be angry. You are part of a group of eleven of the most influential people in the world."

"I'll thank you later. I need to calm down first." George lit and puffed aggressively on his cigar, then finished his glass. It was refilled.

"You did better than anyone expected. Well done and welcome."

"Are there any other rituals I should be aware of?"

"None. You've passed with flying colors."

"And if I failed?"

"You know the consequences. This Order is a double-edged sword. You get the world, but you lose your soul. You can't leave. We make up for it by doing good things. I think you'll agree that our impact on the world has only been good."

George wasn't listening. "I have a child?"

"Oh, that was a bit of a stretch. I'm sorry about that. We wanted to throw you and see what you did with the information."

"So I'm not a father?"

"I'm sorry, Mr. Anderson. Jasmine died tragically in a training exercise in Germany last month. She was never pregnant. You aren't a father."

George sat back, unsure how he felt. He was alive when he was ready to die. He was a father and now wasn't. He didn't know which was worse.

The cigar was his favorite, a Cohiba Siglio VI. The scotch was fifty-year-old Glenfarclas. He was a member of the most secretive and powerful group in the world, an Order that held presidents and CEOs as puppets to its will. He was rich.

He raised his glass to Rock and Roth without saying a word. They did the same.

∞

The next two years were a blur of fame and fortune combining to create a dream life for George. His net worth rose to five billion dollars. He returned to the private sector as the owner of a private American-chartered bank. His clients included the rich and famous from around the world who wanted the discretion and security that his bank provided. For those who didn't want to entangle themselves in American legislation, he directed them to his independent Swiss bank, where he was able to offer an even more discrete service.

He learned that Barbie was right about Swiss finishing schools. There were plenty of wealthy woman who learned how to be the perfect host for him. He was able to combine beauty, youth, and wisdom in his choice of partners. He never found love, but that was something he learned to live without.

His parents flew to every major opening or award and he began to believe that this new reality was his to enjoy. He had the best that life could offer. His business increasingly became that of mergers or acquisitions by his clients. He loved the intricacy of the work and the personalities behind the deals. Money had long ceased to be a concern.

"Look, George, Enron is keen to do the deal. You can't argue about the covenant of Enron. It's blue chip, for god's sake."

"I know what you're saying," George said. "But my client is not prepared to take their stock. We don't want to stand in the way of this deal, but we'll need to see cash or stock of a company my client will accept."

"Who's your client? A Martian?"

"I want to do the deal. You want to do the deal. My client wants to do the deal. It's only an extra hundred million. There must be that kind of cash floating around."

"You want cash. Soon, everyone will want cash."

"I'm not talking about everyone, Mike, just me and my client."

"You're a sonofabitch, you know that? Underneath your five thousand dollar suits and fancy women, you're a cold-hearted lizard like the rest of us."

"Nice to know you care. So, do you think this is a deal-breaker?"

"Naw. I just wanted to drag your ass over here and show you what real work looks like. I know it's hard to leave your princess. What's her name?"

"You know her name," George said. He couldn't stop smiling.

"Anyway, I'm meeting with Arthur Anderson after this and we'll find the money. You want to grab something when I'm done?"

"Sounds like a plan. I haven't had breakfast. I'll drop down to street level and grab something. When and where?"

"Wait a second. Penny, is tomorrow the twelfth?"

"Don't you know your daughter's birthday? September 12. Memorize it. I already got her a present. She'll be eleven tomorrow."

"I know, who would've thought it? Already 2001. We were told the world was going to end with the millennium bug. No such luck."

"Great view," George said, ignoring the banter. "If I worked here, I'd stare out the windows all day."

"Hundred and fourth floor. Hard to get any higher."

"Best view of New York."

"So, George, are we done? Do we have a deal?"

"Yeah, if it's cash, it's a done deal." He was staring into the distance, absorbed by an object coming towards him.

"Shake on it and you can go. It's not even nine in the morning. Haven't you heard that breakfast is for wimps?"

George laughed as they shook hands. Mike gripped his forearm as he did so. Out of the corner of his eye, George saw movement. He turned to look straight out and Mike did the same. They saw a plane flying straight towards them. There was no way for it to change course. George was the only one who said anything before it made impact.

"Oh shit."

ABOUT THE AUTHOR

Baron was born in Canada.
He currently lives in South East England,
somewhere near the Surry/Sussex borders.
Sightings vary.

If you'd like to follow Baron and receive free samples
of his future writing before it is published, please visit
www.baronalexanderbooks.com